Olivia,
Thank you
the support
what mist
would you
Mick

MISTAKES
I MADE DURING
THE ZOMBIE APOCALYPSE

MICHELLE KILMER

Dedicated to friends who have come and gone.
To those I miss and to those I am happier without.

Our triumphs shape us.

Our mistakes, equally so.

CONTENTS

HOW I LEARNED TO KEEP CALM AND LOVE THE APOCALYPSE: AN INTRODUCTION

By T.J. Tranchell

Soon, you will read this line: "Did I wait too long?" In many ways, that question captures the essence of Michelle Kilmer's work. Her stories are filled with people who must take action but often wait too long. Even just a split second can mean the difference between surviving another day or becoming one more member of the shuffling and staggering herd of hungry zombies.

When the zombies come—and in Michelle's world, it is not *if* but *when*—we'll all have to make choices. To act or wait? To fight or give in?

The best zombie tales make us ask how we would react and while we think we know, we don't really know. Those of you who just looked to a corner or a closet, reminding yourself that you have a bug-out bag think you know, but do you?

Since none of us can accurately predict how we will react during the early stages of a zombie apocalypse (and if we're lucky, the late stages), we turn to fiction to help us sort out the possibilities. Then we get to tell ourselves we'd do what a certain hero does and not do what those who succumb too soon did.

Sometimes, the heroes get lucky. Maybe they can answer our first question with a yes, they waited too long. Things could have been different.

I could have saved you.

• • •

The hardest questions are the ones with no answers. The questions that breed self-doubt: why did I survive? What could I have done to save my loved ones? Why don't I just give up? These questions aren't limited to the zombie apocalypse and that is why we keep writing and reading these stories.

Michelle puts these questions right in your face and doesn't back down. In her previous novel *When the Dead*, she lets a small group of survivors ask each other these questions. Sometimes, the hits are worse than a bullet to the brain. Why did *you* survive?

Survivor's guilt can crush your soul, even if you managed to keep your body alive. You are a zombie: a walking corpse with no purpose other than to consume. It is no way to live a life.

And that, unfortunately, is the truth so many zombie stories neglect. Too many offer the hope of a cure or that society will rebuild. Michelle's brand of hope is much more realistic. She knows we're all fucked. There is no way back from this level of chaos. The world will be fundamentally different and surviving will be about changing, not trying to make things the way they were before.

With change comes mistakes.

• • •

Every writer makes mistakes. We sometimes put characters in situations that don't make sense and have them do things that are not "true" in the context of the character. If we're lucky, the characters will show us what we did wrong. It takes time and practice to be able to see these mistakes as a writer. The novice throws whatever they think on the page and lets it ride. And then they wonder why no one will publish their stories or buy their books.

This isn't bad; it just means that writer—much like the protagonist of the book you now hold—needs to slow down and reconsider their actions. You might be thinking that slowing down in the middle of the zombie apocalypse but remember where we started. "Did I wait too long?" also requires us to ask if we moved too soon. We can't have all action, all the time, as the saying goes. Michelle, even in her need to propel the story, gives us time to contemplate why certain actions were taken just long enough to forget that danger is about to come crashing back in. It is a rare skill to convince a reader that even though nothing will be fine, that there is still a reason to live.

We all make mistakes. That doesn't mean we are hopeless lost causes. It means we need to keep calm and fight the good fight. Michelle Kilmer is a fighter, a survivor. She fights to bring you the best tales of the apocalypse that she can. Her characters make plenty of mistakes along the way because we all do.

Buying this book wasn't a mistake on your part, dear reader. If this isn't your first foray into Michelle Kilmer's work, you already know that. If *Mistakes I Made During the Zombie Apocalypse* is your first Michelle Kilmer book, by the end you will be asking yourself why you waited so long.

Don't wait any more. Start reading.

T.J. Tranchell
Moscow, Idaho
September 12, 2015

MISTAKES
I MADE DURING
THE ZOMBIE APOCALYPSE

MICHELLE KILMER

...I GAVE UP ON LIFE

In the middle of a uniquely busy city, on a once quiet street, on the second floor of a mostly abandoned house, in a bedroom's small closet, Ian Ward is sitting alone. Even if anyone else in the city were still alive, there wouldn't be room for them in his tiny hiding place.

There are any number of things Ian is hiding from. Keller Kenton, for one; the asshole that burned his real house down and sent Lena to ruin his life. And the zombies, of course. Those who valued their lives (and a small part of Ian still did) would make sure to hide from them. But mostly he is hiding from something downstairs that he doesn't want to believe is there.

It *is* there. And we'll get to that.

His life, if it can be called living, has been reduced to scrounging for food from anywhere he can; scraps from long forgotten trashcans and crumbs from dirty kitchen floors have become his sustenance. This too is all dependent on if he has the guts and strength to leave the closet, which most of Ian no longer does.

His life sucks.

Outside of the house, in the streets and filling the buildings, hundreds of thousands of the undead have taken over. Because of this, Ian's thoughts often jump back and forth between finding his next meal and making sure he isn't someone else's.

Like a caveman, he thinks. No time to relax. Only survive.

• • •

And what does survival mean anyway?
"It really only means that your heart is still beating," Ian answers
himself. He presses a pillow to his face and, for a second,
considers leaving it there until his heart is no longer beating.

But then you'd be a zombie stuck in a closet. That's even worse.
"It would be a fitting punishment," he says because he believes he
is a waste of air.

• • •

He screams into the sweat-stained thing. It helps to muffle
the sound. It helps to release some of the anger that keeps bottling
up inside of him.

At 17 he is nearly an adult and after what he did a few days
ago, any lingering spark of childish thought and deed has most
definitely left him. No child, no kind-hearted innocent would do
something like *that*.

What is it that he did, you ask?

He won't let me tell you yet. He isn't quite ready to talk about
it. He has barely accepted it as true. He thinks that *it* will walk into
the room any minute now, erasing what happened.

From his solitary post in the closet, Ian is attempting to self-
treat so as not to develop any form of psychosis. This is something
his psychologist father would strongly advise against, but his father
is dead. Even when he was alive he was useless at his job anyway,
always pissing off clients with his haughty attitude and causing
more harm than good. Ian doesn't know the symptoms to watch
for, the tendencies. He only knows the word psychosis because
his dad threw it around like a badge of authority or a weighted
stopwatch to get someone to shut up. If any of his father's books
had survived the fire, he could refer to those, but Keller was
thorough in his destruction. It truly was the blind leading the blind.

The house that holds his closet hadn't looked too bad from
the outside when he and his best friend Grant came upon it a week
ago. It was two stories with a double garage and a well-kept lawn
and it had none of the warning signs that said bad things awaited
them inside. That was what Ian's brain remembered, but he had
beheld it with starvation in his belly and the dead at his back.

It turned out to be a shithole. Mice or rats have eaten
holes through the sheetrock at the base of the walls, dust covers

everything. The water probably didn't run before it stopped running in the rest of the city. If Ian ever goes back outside, he won't recognize the building from which he came out.

He wants you to know that he is stronger than this. Or that he thought he was. That he was going to *survive* and he sure as hell wasn't going to "keep a journal." Not even a few notes on a scrap of paper. Ian never planned to become a lonely teenage boy writing beautiful and disturbing things about his final days. His mom might have told you that he is a "fancy fabricator" and a "king of lies", and those things were true at a time, but he wants you to know and believe that this is all true. He wouldn't *want* to make this shit up. And any past lie was probably a result of Grant's influence; not part of Ian's natural build. That doesn't matter anymore. Nothing matters.

But here he is, using an empty calorie counting journal and a pen that Grant stole from Walgreens to keep the journal he said he wouldn't. Mind you, he won't be counting calories. There are few overeaters in the apocalypse. And he is using me to tell you all of this because he's too chickenshit to tell it himself.

• • •

"This is the only way I know how," Ian says, his voice quavering.
To tell your story as though you are someone else?
"Maybe it will become my own again. When the pain lessens."

• • •

Earlier today one of the many newly-stray cats found its way into Ian's mostly abandoned house. It poked around first in the kitchen, but no crumbs were to be found as Ian ate them all several days ago. The cat, a fluffy calico missing its collar, jumped gracefully over the old pool of coagulated blood and the body in the doorway to the hall. It sniffed the air, a curious mix of metal and old, rotting meat, but again found nothing of interest.

• • •

How do you know what the cat did before it came to you?
"What do you mean?" Ian asks aloud.
This is your *story. You can't know what you didn't see.*

"You just said it. This is *my* story. I'll tell it however I want to."
At least you still have some fight in you. Go on.

• • •

Ms. Kitty—as Ian dubbed it and its missing tag might have labeled it—walked slowly up the stairs to the second floor and easily followed the scent of spectacularly aged tuna to a spot in the wall that she knew would open if she complained enough. She searched for her most pitiful voice and let out a *merow*.

Ian jumped at the sound.

The wall did not open, but she heard movement on the other side and so she *merowed* again, this time with more urgency, something she hoped the being could hear in her voice.

A fucking cat! Ian thought. He hated cats, especially when the fleas from this cat's mangy body crawled under the door to bite his legs.

"Kitty!" Ian whispered as quietly as he could. "Shut up!"

A human. Ms. Kitty was happy about that. The other ones tried to grab her and they never shared their food or talked to her, but this one was different. She began to purr.

"Why do you things always find me?" Ian asked, knowing full well it was because he couldn't stand them and that, in some way, drew them to him.

Still the cat wailed at the top of its little cat lungs.

The dead followed noise with an instinctual passion, regardless of its source. The cat would get Ian killed if it didn't close its stupid cat mouth. He tucked his pants into his socks, stood up in the small space and slowly opened the door. As he made his way to the bedroom window, Ms. Kitty followed close to him, rubbing her filthy body against his legs.

They love this, she remembered.

"Stop that, I fucking hate it!" Ian whispered, but he didn't push the cat away. His plan involved it and the ten zombies down on the front lawn. Grant would have wrung the cat's neck, because he was a problem solver, but Ian was only really learning how to manage now and he wouldn't kill unless he absolutely…had to.

• • •

Is it time to tell them?
"No way, no fucking way."
Ian's heart is pounding, pulling the remaining energy from the
rest of his body to express his anxiety. For a moment, he feels
bad about what he did to the cat, but then he scratches at the
fleabites still plaguing his ankles.
What did you do to that nasty thing?

• • •

Ian opened the latch on the window and swung it open. The
air was crisp and surprisingly fresh. The night, still. No wind blew
which meant that Ms. Kitty's mournful wails were easier for the
undead to hear. He held his hand out to the four-legged monster
and it hungrily walked closer for more love.

Next comes the food, Ms. Kitty thought.

Ian quickly slid one hand under the cat's belly and with a
fluid arc of his arm he sent the cat flying out the window into the
yard below. It landed on its feet and the dead swarmed it, but the
cat was too quick. It scrambled into some bushes on the left side
of the lawn.

Now, hours later, Ian is back in the closet discovering more
fleabites with the beam of his dying flashlight and trying to regain
body heat lost to the fall air. A few pieces of musty clothing that
were never glamorous or nice are piled atop him. The dust and
a cold developing in his chest drive him to cough. He presses a
thick, wool coat against his mouth to maintain his invisibility to
the dead. Its fabric houses countless moth larvae. In his hacking,
Ian has accidentally inhaled some. He nearly wretches, but reminds
himself to be thankful for the eighth-cup of squirming protein.
There are two sleeping bags in the room beyond the closet door,
but he refuses to allow himself such luxury.

As his body and the closet warm up, the smell from what he
left downstairs is returning. He climbed in the closet to get away
from that mess, but it keeps creeping back into his nose and his
mind.

His father wouldn't like to hear about his avoidance or the "reduced activity" of his closet life. He'd tell Ian that he had a serious disorder. Ian would have to agree. His was the first documented case of "post-apocalypsia." Then Ian would laugh and his father would yell at him for making fun of mental health. Ian shouldn't take mental health lightly because something is definitely wrong with him. Dreaming up conversations with dead relatives could be viewed as delusional.

• • •

"I don't know if he's dead," Ian says to himself.

No, you don't. But if you were being honest with yourself, you'd admit that your father was never cut out to survive. Arthur Ward would be the guy trying to reason with a zombie as it bit into the flesh of his arm.

"You're right. He'd be psychoanalyzing and diagnosing anger issues and suggesting treatment all the way to his grave."

• • •

Back to the things of which we are certain. The bedroom beyond the closet isn't completely empty. It has a nice bed; one of those big, well-made four-poster beds. It would block the door well, but Ian doesn't have enough strength to move it. And anyway, blockading doesn't work if the dead find out you're inside. They will tear at the wall until they make a new hole to tear at you through.

Speaking of things tearing at people, Ian is ready to tell you why he is worthless and alone and unable to cope with anything.

• • •

Ian? Do share.

He clears his drying throat to speak aloud.

"I am worthless and alone because…"

...I KILLED MY BEST FRIEND

"Downstairs in this house, below where I am sitting."

• • •

The metallic scent of blood wafts up through the stairwell. For Ian, killing undead Grant was different than killing the other zombies, and not because they were friends. Grant was *angrier* and his eyes drilled into Ian as he attacked, as though he was aware of all that had transpired. This eerie awareness of Ian's shortcomings was actually guilt that filled Ian. His freshly undead friend was truly *just* a zombie with only one need or care, to feed. But guilt is a powerful thing.

Even though hardly a week has passed, his memories of the living Grant have faded quickly. When people you love are alive and reachable for an afternoon conversation, it's easy to think of all the times you've been together and all of the fun you've had on other occasions. But as soon as they have left the living world, only tidbits of their life and what they meant to you bubble to the surface of your memory. It might be a unique gesture, an oft-repeated phrase, or a scent that clung to them. Ian is having difficulty remembering any of it.

In an effort to recall something more than Grant's anger in the end, Ian pulls his legs in tight, rests his forehead on his knees and wraps his arms around his body. He closes his eyes and searches his memory.

• • •

Tell us, Ian. What did your best friend look like?

"He had very dark hair, blacker than black if that is possible," Ian says into the darkness. "He rarely washed it. It was oily and shiny, like crow feathers. He was tall. My Mom measured us both at our house since Grant's mom didn't do nice things. He had five inches on me. The features of his face were chiseled. When he smiled, lines formed at the corners of his mouth. He could pass for 25. I think his fake id said that anyway. He used it for beer."

• • •

Grant had been handsome before he was dead. More handsome than Ian. The girls at school chased Grant, but always regretted it. They labeled him a "jerk" or a "total asshole." He was loyal only to Ian. Ian, with an extra twenty pounds on his waistline, was not the pick of the litter, but he was a much nicer person than his friend. Regardless, the girls he liked never liked him back. You might get a half decent guy if you combined Ian's personality with Grant's body. Separate they were nothing, which is partially why surviving without him was extra difficult for Ian.

He lost half of himself when Grant died, when he killed him.

• • •

How did you kill him, Ian? We're supposed to be talking about that. You won't make any progress if you avoid the story. How did it start?
"I was sitting next to his body, waiting for it to move again."

• • •

Grant had been killed once and now he would rise again. How quickly Grant would turn, Ian wasn't sure. There wasn't a science to it as far as he knew. So he sat down on the floor near him and looked around at the shitty house in which his best friend had just died. There on the floor, Ian could feel a draft of cold air coming under the back door. He got to his feet, grabbed the dusty tablecloth from the unused dining room and rolled it into a long tube. It fit the breezy gap well and helped cut down on the wind significantly.

They had talked many times in the past about the proper way to kill one another in the event of infection. A blade of any kind was too personal and messy. Both agreed on a gunshot wound to the brain, effective and easiest for the living party. Only Ian hated guns and he didn't have one anyway. Any gun they'd found was useless to them.

• • •

So, you were going to leave him? Let him rise and walk alone, forever in this house?

"I knew there had to be a better house than this one, maybe even in the same neighborhood. But it was cold outside and getting colder. I was scared of going out with no one to watch my back."

You decided to stay and take care of it.

"He would have done the same for me. I needed to find something to re-kill him with."

• • •

Ian wandered the first floor of the house in search of a weapon that would be easy to wield and tough enough to break a skull with minimal effort. This would have been a normal time for him to cry, but he was in shock and there was still work to be done, so he had to stay focused. He opted for a leg from one of the dining room chairs. The dining set was one of the few nice things in the house, made of solid hardwood, not flat pack crap from Ikea. He tried repeatedly to break a leg off. Sheer force could not compromise the quality and construction of the chair. In the basement, Ian located a wrench to loosen the nut that held the leg. The wrench itself could have been a better weapon from an impact standpoint but he couldn't tolerate being closer to zombie Grant than necessary. He'd need the full length of the chair leg between them.

He returned with the weapon in time for Grant's reanimation.

The chair leg felt great in his hands, sturdy, but he wished for more time to increase its lethality. There were nails and barbed wire in the basement. He could get the taxidermied elk head that was still embedded in the other body in a sitting room down the hall, but it was slippery with blood.

• • •

You killed more time than zombies that day.

"I really didn't want to come up with ways to destroy my best friend's brain."

A sharp pain travels up from his hands and into his arms.

You're clenching your fists. You're drawing blood.
Ian brings awareness to his fingers. Indeed the nails at the ends
of them are digging into the skin of his palms. He opens his
hands and wipes the blood on his pants.
*The fleas will love you for this easy feast. Now, we were killing Grant,
weren't we?*

• • •

It took five blows and he managed to get them all in before
Grant could stand up. Panting and sobbing, Ian stood and let the
chair leg drop to the hallway floor.

Normal people would have moved the body, would have
tried to keep the house livable. Normal people would have bagged
the pieces and scrubbed the blood from the floorboards. Grant
and Ian, together, would have, but Ian wasn't himself anymore and
Grant was a lump of non-moving flesh and bone.

The smell gets stronger every day, reminding Ian that decay
happens and although the house was cold with winter air, it wasn't
cold enough to slow the process much. Necessity doesn't make
killing someone less horrific. A set of biting teeth doesn't make
bashing a head in less likely to scar someone for the remainder of
their life. When Ian fell asleep in the closet on the first night after
dealing with Grant, he dreamt of the sound of the wood hitting
his head and the gurgling noises that came from his throat as it
filled with blood.

The images and sounds fit nicely into his growing library of
nightmares.

• • •

You aren't telling them everything, Ian.
"What am I leaving out?" he screams. "He's gone! Nothing's
going to bring him back!"
*It's the second time you killed him. Tell them why his eyes held so much anger
toward you.*
"He had every right to be angry with me! He died in the first
place because…"

...I DIDN'T PLAY HERO

In every house they'd had the pleasure of occupying, Ian and Grant had a rule about keeping all of the interior doors open. It was important to leave oneself as many exits from a room as possible. With a vicious zombie on your toes, every moment was precious. Earlier, on the night he ended up dead, Grant heard noises from the first floor of the shitty house. Bravely, or stupidly, he crawled from his sleeping bag and went downstairs to find the cause.

• • •

You are telling someone else's story again.
"It's important. I can't understand my mistakes if I don't examine the mistakes of others."
Don't blame Grant for this. Especially when you are getting to the part where you failed him.
"He could have stayed upstairs."
You could have done a lot of things.

• • •

Ian awoke when he heard the creaking of the stairs. He remembered that they weren't alone. When he saw that Grant wasn't in his sleeping bag he left the warmth of his own to follow after his friend.

"Why are all the doors closed and where did this blood come from?" Grant asked him from the first floor hallway. A delicate trail of crimson droplets led from room to room and Grant now had it on his feet. Ian stood on the stairs, staring down at him over the railing. He knew the answer to both parts of Grant's question. *The girl* had closed the doors; the girl who was covered in bleeding wounds who he never found a moment to tell Grant about, she was the only one who could have.

• • •

23

Why did she close the doors?
"I don't know. She must have been trying to keep the heat in or the shadows-turned-monsters out. Maybe it was Keller's idea?"
You are transferring blame to someone else again. You know this is your fault. You didn't do enough.
"I called to him. I remember saying something!" Ian yells as he slams a fist against the closet door. It sends a shudder through the walls of the house and dust falls down from the ceiling.
Calm down and tell them what you said.

• • •

"Come back to bed," Ian whispered, choosing to ignore answering Grant's questions. He needed to get Grant back upstairs before the girl woke up and he found out about her.

"'Come to bed?' That's some *Brokeback Mountain* shit," Grant said with a laugh.

It was all Ian had. What else could he have said without giving away the girl?

"That's not what I meant," he clarified.

"Whatever you meant, I'm not coming. How the hell will I be able to fall asleep again when the floors are covered in blood? Someone's in the house! Don't you care?"

Ian cared about many things still. He cared not to piss off his friend, he cared to find enough food each day, that he and Grant would get out of this hellhole of a house and find a better place to survive and he absolutely cared that he had finally lost his virginity. But it did not matter to him for Grant to follow a blood trail that would lead him to another of Ian's poor decisions.

• • •

"Grant didn't have to follow the blood," Ian told the fleas that he hadn't yet managed to crush with his overgrown fingernails. "He could have waited."

But the bloody girl couldn't wait, could she? She introduced herself.
"She came up behind him and even though it was dark, I knew something was different with her. Because he was tall, he towered over her, but the plague made her appear larger somehow

24

and more frightening. I opened my mouth to warn him, but a
floorboard creaked as she shifted her weight. He turned slowly
until they were face to face."

• • •

"Where the fuck did this bitch come from?" Grant asked Ian
without taking his eyes off of her shadowy form. He was confused
because the doors were closed and zombies didn't turn doorknobs.

A full moon cast a beam of light in through a window above
the back door. The girl unintentionally moved into the glow. Grant
asked again where the girl had come from. Ian, too scared to make
more noise, cursed at himself in his head and didn't answer.

• • •

You didn't have to talk, you had other choices, but you got hung up on words.
"What could I have done? Jumped the railing and landed on her
back? Told Grant to run and try to distract her while we found
weapons?" Ian argues with himself, throwing his hands up in the
dark of the closet in a passionate defense of his inaction.
*Those are both very good options. The house is full of weapons, if you are
looking for them.*
"Well, I know that now!"

• • •

Behind closed door number one there was a dull butcher
knife in an old knife block on the kitchen counter. Its handle
already stained with a bit of red, though it was dried tomato that
had never been washed off. Behind double doors numbers two
and three, a coat rack tucked into a corner by the front door. Either
end would be effective, with multiple prongs. In fact it had been
used as a weapon twice before. The previous homeowners were an
unhappy couple and the woman found it the perfect tool to wail on
her husband after late night boozing.

Door number four led to the basement and a heavy wrench
that would have worked well for the task of beating in the girl's
brains. The drunken husband had once considered the same thing
for his wife, but fell asleep and sobered up before acting on the
impulse.

A chair from the dining room behind door number five could have kept the bloody girl at a safe distance until one of the other weapons was retrieved.

Grant, alone in this event as his friend was completely worthless, saw two possible options, neither of which involved weapons or Ian. Both involved closed doors. He could run head on into the infected girl and take a moment to open a door into a room that she'd follow him into. Or, he could take the door at the end of the hall, behind him, that opened to the backyard.

The backyard. Its fence, which of course was a work of utter shit when it was first built, hadn't kept anything out or even stood mostly upright for over ten years. The yard sat against a wooded area and beyond that, a major shopping center. Now, the backyard was full of zombies.

It was a mystery to them as to why she hadn't attacked yet. Ian watched Grant stand there, still, as though—like a dinosaur of some kind—she wouldn't see him unless he moved. But she could definitely see him and she was going to kill him. Like any other predator, she simply wanted a taste of the hunt. Her hungry eyes bore into him, daring him to run.

You may have heard the term 'dumbstruck' or 'awestruck' to describe an inability to act or even move because fear, beauty or extraordinary circumstances stop someone in their tracks. At that moment, Ian was experiencing this feeling for the first time. As he saw the girl's changed face in the moonlight, he was unable to do anything but stare. She was still as beautiful as when he'd first met her. She hadn't attacked anyone yet, meaning her face was clean and not covered in the blood and gore of others. Her eyes hadn't sunken in or gone milky or discolored with decay.

• • •

"I couldn't stop looking at her."

You're thinking of her even now.

"She was more beautiful dead than she was alive."

Ever since you lost your virginity to the other girl, it's all you think about.

"I don't want to think about *her*," Ian says. Tears begin to drop like bombshells onto the wool coat in his lap and the moth larvae there.

Tell them more about this girl then.

• • •

Her face was relaxed and there was no hint of the attitude with which she'd come in. Her skin was a smooth, porcelain plain. The wounds that covered her body no longer seeped blood, as her heart was still. She was the calm before the storm.

Her beauty, too, moved Grant, but he stayed unmoving due to a paralyzing fear. The beast was before him. He muttered Ian's name just loud enough for him to hear it. The girl let out a hiss or yowl comparable to a large cat sending a warning signal to potential prey. It was low and wet.

Hearing it, Grant decided it was time to move or die. He turned to his right and reached for the kitchen doorknob. She jumped on him and they fell into the passage between the hall and kitchen.

"Ian! Ian!" he yelled, over and over.

• • •

"And still, I stood there."

You stood there and watched it happen. Didn't even descend one single step.

• • •

Not until Ian saw a wash of blood on his friend's arms did he regain awareness of the situation. Suddenly the sounds of flesh tearing and the smacking of the girl's feeding lips filled his ears. He took a step down the stairs, but again froze, remembering that he was weaponless. And despite the fact that she was satisfying her hunger, the killer in her was still on high alert. If she heard him, she would attack him as voraciously as she had Grant.

In mere minutes his best friend, whom he'd known since he was three, had bled completely out. As though she could tell he had expired, the girl stopped devouring his flesh. She wandered away down the hall, leaving Grant's body to rot like a forgotten plate of no longer desirable food.

Crying on the stairs seemed like a good idea. Grant was

his last friend, and again if Ian was being realistic, his *only* friend. But now a killing machine walked the first floor and he'd seen the undead scramble up stairs before. He had to take care of her before she realized another perfectly edible person was nearby.

He carefully made his way to the bottom of the stairs and, judging by the trail of bloody footprints she left, the girl was in the sitting room. What a zombie would do in a sitting room did not concern Ian, but he was *very* interested in the mounted elk head in the living room across the hall.

• • •

"You forgot to list it as a weapon."
I didn't want to give your story away. Besides, I already mentioned it. Go on…

• • •

Ian lifted the hunting trophy from the wall and, though it was stuffed, it weighed nearly fifty pounds. He hefted it and ran at the girl, whose back was turned to him. One of the horns slipped easily into her flesh and he used his momentum to push her against the wall of the sitting room. Still she tried to bite him, craning her neck without respect for the vertebrae in it. Ian had no qualms or queasiness. He could no longer see her beauty, only her evil. Her face was caked with bits of Grant's flesh and smeared with his blood. It sent him into a rage.

He jammed the horn deeper into her body and moved it up and down to rip her apart. Then he pulled away and shook the elk head to remove her from the horn. Though her body had several holes in it, she moved to attack once more. He tripped her and stood on top of her, his feet sinking into her gut. From this position of power, he dropped the elk head on her skull. Her intestines were squishing up between his toes, but all he wanted was for her to stop glaring at him. He picked up the head again and made sure to send a horn into her brain.

Ian fell to the side of her body. His feet wore a layer of excrement and newly rotting insides. He held his head, panting and crying and trying to avoid looking at his feet. Instead, he observed something on the girl's wrist. Below the scars and wounds that would never heal, she was wearing a bracelet made with silver beads. Four of the beads had letters engraved on them. He turned them to reveal the name. L-E-N-A. He didn't know how to pronounce it since she'd never told him her name. Lee-na, Lay-na. It might even have been short for Helena, or maybe a name he'd never heard of as parents were naming their kids all kinds of weird names these days.

• • •

"Her name doesn't matter."

Then you should tell them, like you told Grant's body, how the bloody girl got inside.

"No one needs to know that."

It might help you get rid of some of the guilt.

"Ha!" Ian laughs. "Nothing but death will take away my guilt."

You must be held accountable for your actions.

He takes a deep breath in, itches a particularly bothersome fleabite on his thigh and begins.

"We had found a place we thought was safe but the reinforced door didn't matter because…"

Michelle Kilmer

...I LET THE WRONG ONE IN

The sun was working its way toward the horizon and Grant and Ian were upstairs in the bedroom of the house, going through what belongings were left between them. It was a grim situation, but they knew that every house in the neighborhood was a potential treasure trove of food and supplies, once they could get to them.

"We'll have to stay inside and let the dead calm down. It could be a couple of days before we're able to sneak around out there." Grant unrolled his sleeping bag on the dusty floor and pulled out his iPod. Little battery remained on the device, but he needed to unwind from what they'd been through earlier that day so he popped the earbuds in and lay down.

Ian set his sleeping bag on the bare mattress of the four-poster bed, but, instead of lying down, he searched the house. *There has to be something of value*, he thought. Two other bedrooms on the second floor, one the master, held little more than the room in which he'd left Grant. The living room, sitting room and dining room downstairs held only old furniture, nothing of real use unless Ian got creative or, later, desperate. The basement was likely to produce something of value, but he wasn't yet willing to venture into its dark recesses alone. The only room left was the kitchen. Ian prepared himself to be let down, especially since there had been another family in the neighborhood capable of raiding the place.

All ten of the counter's built-in drawers were empty and he checked five cupboards before he found anything still edible. The sixth cupboard's two shelves held four cans of soup. He held one in his hand. The expiration date was difficult to make out, but the can wasn't dented or bloated. They would feast tonight! He was about to grab the other cans and bring them to Grant when a soft knock came on the front door.

Ian closed the cupboard. It seemed ominous that an outsider would find them just as they found food. He couldn't let someone take their supplies again, but his curiosity won out. He went to the heavy drapes of the living room and glanced outside. A beautiful girl, covered in small, bleeding cuts, was standing on the front porch. He watched her for a while, hoping she would leave.

• • •

Ian can feel the anger growing in him.
"She didn't leave."
She knocked again.
"Who knocks during the fucking apocalypse?" Ian asks, hitting himself in the head for being so dumb and not doubting it when it happened.

• • •

It was true. No one knocked on doors anymore, not even the Mormons. You entered without announcement or invitation and then you suffered the consequences if there were consequences to be suffered.

• • •

"She knew we were there, because Keller sent her to destroy us."
He might have been an arsonist and an asshole, but Keller wasn't that clever or convincing.

• • •

She knocked a third time. She had no visible weapons and her face was streaked with tears. Grant was overly concerned about contamination and if he had been down there with Ian, he wouldn't have let her in. He would have told the girl to spend the night on the porch. They both knew that time would always answer the question of whether someone was infected or not. In the morning, they would either have another walking corpse or a new, albeit beat up, friend. And though one was preferable to another, they were both another mouth to feed. Deciding to minimize risk, as many decisions in the apocalypse were about, Ian opened a window first.

"Are you okay?" he asked her quietly.

She jumped, startled by the sudden noise from within the

house. She shook her head 'no' and began crying again. "I've lost everything and I'm hurt."

The last part wasn't a necessary addition to her sentence. Ian could see that she had injuries. He looked at the front yard behind her and the street beyond. No sign of others, but he and Grant had walked into well-laid traps before.

• • •

"How could I have been so stupid?"

Give yourself a break. She was cute; much cuter than the other girls.

"Those fucking girls," Ian says, remembering a trio they'd met before coming to the house.

Don't think about them now. We're telling Lena's story.

• • •

Unlike the "fucking girls", Lena was throwing up red flags that Ian should have seen. But ever since he'd been unable to save the girl he'd slept with, he was feeling the need for heroics; an honest chance to redeem himself. Her endless crying only helped her case. He opened the door slowly and let her in. He waited for a surprise attack, a bombing without a warning siren, a silent bullet to his head, but nothing happened so he closed the door. The girl had already walked herself to a couch in the living room, where her leaking blood was working on staining the upholstery.

"What happened to you?" he asked her, eyeing the cuts that covered her body. They didn't seem like injuries caused by the dead. Zombies took chunks out of your flesh, not precise cuts evenly spaced across the epidermis. Anyone not blinded by testosterone would see that a steady human hand had done the damage.

• • •

You're writing Keller into this again. I can tell.

"She was just like the walking Molotovs he sent. A bomb waiting to explode."

But that isn't what she told you.

• • •

"I got chased through blackberry bushes," she said. But many of the wounds were deeper than anything a thorn might cause. Of course Ian didn't press the issue.

"Those look infected." The skin around the cuts was red and inflamed. "You can clean up in the bathroom down the hall and sleep here, on the couch."

Her eyes widened. "Why can't I stay upstairs away from the big windows?"

He wanted to hide her from Grant because he'd put her straight back out in the cold. And she couldn't know about Grant either. If she wasn't dying, she'd choose him over Ian. If he kept Grant a secret, he might actually have a chance with this girl.

"They can't see you when the curtains are closed," Ian pointed out, hoping the weak reason would hold up against her fear, fake or not.

She walked toward the curtains. "They'll hear me," she whimpered.

"Don't let them," Ian warned. Her silence would be doubly beneficial. "There's some food in the kitchen but you'll have to eat it cold." He walked to the stairs.

"You act like you own this place," she said. The attitude caught Ian by surprise. He'd just offered her room and board, though it was a first-floor couch and cold food.

"I do own it now. It's a buyer's market."

• • •

You didn't say that to her. You aren't that clever.

"I know, but I came up with it later."

You can't just add whatever you want to the story. They'll stop believing you.

"I'll do whatever the fuck I want!" Ian shrieks. His throat is dry from talking. He reaches around the closet to find his last water bottle and then takes a swig.

When you are ready, tell them what you really said.

• • •

"I hate this house. It should be burned to the ground." As soon as the words came out of his mouth, he regretted them. If the girl was working for Keller, she already knew about his pyromania. She might even have a lighter and gasoline in her backpack.

34

• • •

"I don't want to talk about her anymore. It's like talking with a ghost. Pointless and painful."

You already told them about what happened to Grant.

"That doesn't mean I'm over it."

This isn't the end of her story, or rather, you haven't finished the beginning yet.

• • •

"Just keep it down okay?" Ian asked. Back upstairs and bundled in his sleeping bag for the night, sleep eluded him. He expected the girl to do something stupid and loud.

Nice guys check on girls, he thought. He also remembered there was some rubbing alcohol in one of the kitchen cabinets. Maybe she could clean her wounds. So he slid out of the sack and crept back downstairs. He checked the living room, but it was empty. On his way back to the stairs, he saw light glowing from the dining room. He walked to the doorway. Lena sat at the end of the dining table. A flashlight stood upright, illuminating the ceiling and room. Her sleeves were pulled up and in one hand she held a razor blade, which she dragged across her arm.

"Whoa."

His voice startled her for a second time that evening, causing her hand to force the blade deeper than she intended.

"Fuck!" Lena yelled. "I thought you went to bed!"

"I wanted to make sure you were alright." Clearly she wasn't. "The cuts, you did them to yourself?"

She didn't answer, but she hung her head in shame.

Ian couldn't understand ruining a body so beautiful. "Why?"

Lena looked up. "I like to see the blood; to know I'm still one of the living. Death doesn't have me yet." Still holding the razor between two fingers, she dabbed another finger in the blood that was seeping out of her and smeared it on her skin.

Ian walked around the table and pulled out the chair next to her. She set the razor blade down. He could see it was rusted and covered in blood both new and old. It belonged in the garbage, not releasing life from her flesh. Now that he was closer he could also see the many raised scars that crossed her forearm in neat rows.

"Those healed a long time ago," Ian said. "Before the dead started walking."

"I needed to know I was alive then too," Lena said, but she offered no more explanation. "So, can you go now?"

"Yeah, I guess. Will you be okay?" he asked. She was pale and sweaty, like she was sick. *Sick* wasn't good in the apocalypse.

Lena shrugged and then motioned her hand to shoo him away.

• • •

A realization pops into Ian's head. "Keller could have dipped her blade in infected blood. She was already infected when I let her in!"

She could have died from a regular infection. You saw the blade. She didn't keep it clean.

• • •

Ian reached the top of the stairs and he remembered something Grant had said a few weeks prior "one day a drop of blood is going to change our lives in a very bad way if we aren't careful". It was bad enough that Ian allowed someone into the house, let alone a bloody someone. He went back to bed and finally fell asleep. In his dreams he completely reimagined the encounter.

Lena wasn't downstairs. She wasn't hurt. She didn't even exist to knock on the door. Ian wasn't incapable of discernment. He had turned away a man that had come to the house earlier that day, not a girl. The man, like the zombies, was skin and bones and his life-worn body moved in a jilted manner. He could have been mistaken for a one of the dead, but when he chose a direct path to the front door and used a bony hand to knock on it, Ian knew him to still be living. Grant was out scavenging so the task of turning away the skeleton fell to Ian.

He opened the door a crack. A locking chain allowed him to see who was there without risking them barging in uninvited.

"Hi," he said. His face was weathered with deep wrinkles

and liver spots. He wore loose overalls and a plaid shirt beneath them. To Ian, who had seen one-too-many horror movies, the man on the porch looked like someone who would eat people or keep fetuses in jars in his basement; like a killer.

"Are you boys doing all right in there?" the man asked with a gravelly voice that rattled around in his chest before leaving his lips.

The old man's question told Ian a lot. He knew that there were two of them and that they were young enough to not be doing well without parents.

"Have you been watching us?" Ian asked. He was worried about what his answer would be because looters weren't uncommon. He could have a list of everything they owned for all he knew. And a shorter list of the items he would take.

"I seen you come and go. Your friend is looking thin," the man said.

"He always looks like that," Ian explained, though his words came out slowly like molasses. Ian thought it strange that a man whose skin was stretched taut over his bones would call someone else thin.

"We don't have enough to share, I'm sorry," he said, remembering the cans of soup in the kitchen cupboard.

"I ain't here for food," he said. "Just checking on you. Must be hard to go through this without your parents."

"They weren't home much anyway, when they were alive." Ian shrugged.

"Knowing you ain't never gonna see them again is different though," the man said as his head dropped. "I've lost a lot of important people in my life, even before all this mess."

"I guess you're right. Hey, look, all the cold air is coming in and the dead are out there." Ian glanced left and right for effect. The old man raised a hand up in goodbye or understanding and turned to take the same path back across the yard.

"Who was that?" Lena asked from behind him.

In the dream he turned to face her and saw that she was

37

covered in blood.

• • •

It's dark out. We should sleep.
Ian remembers his sleeping bag, which is still out on the bare
mattress of the four-poster bed. He is too tired to get it and so
he falls asleep in the closet, under the musty coat in the mostly
abandoned house. He dreams that Grant's corpse is sitting in the
closet with him, listening to every word of Ian's recollections and
shaking his head in disgust.

• • •

The next day he wakes up shivering. He stands up and moves his
legs in place to get his heart pumping faster. Grant's lifeless body
is downstairs where it should be.
Good morning, sunshine.
Somewhere in the dark of the closet there is a small Tupperware
with the last drops of juice from a can of pineapple he'd eaten
days before. It had been his last meal, the only food he had left.
Ian finds the juice and drinks it down in one small gulp. The
tartness shocks him and the sugary liquid makes his teeth hurt,
but still he savors the meager breakfast. There's soup downstairs,
but he still cannot bear to step over Grant's body to get it.
*Now that you've done your morning routine of nothing, tell them how you
ended up here.*
"We wouldn't have been stuck in this horrible place or crossed
paths with Lena except that…"

...I DIDN'T HAVE A BACKUP PLAN

"And it cost the Cohens their lives."

• • •

Days prior, with nowhere safe to go and only a few supplies left in their pockets, Grant and Ian were running out of options. They made it twenty blocks before the crowd of the undead was too dense to safely pass through. It was time to lay low for a while and it was easy enough to tell which houses to avoid. The blood-smeared windows were an obvious *Do Not Enter* sign. Wide open doors meant anything could be lurking in the halls. And in some of the houses they could just plain see zombies wandering within. The neighborhood they were in had been truly decimated, with a mix of the warning signs above, leaving little choice as to where they could hide.

"Over there!" Grant yelled, pointing to a one story blue house, with perfect white trim and a picket fence. It was the only house on the block left untouched by the dead. There were several zombies on the front lawn, but they looked to be completely unmoving, like statues made of slowly melting flesh. Ian saw a last name on the mailbox as they ran past it. *Cohen*, it read. At the door, the boys were elated to find it unlocked.

There were many things they hoped to find in the blue house with perfect white trim. Cupboards full of canned food, clean beds to sleep in, a fenced backyard, and a basement stocked with weapons. The house had all of those things.

It also had a family still living in it.

"What the hell are you doing in my house?" A tall man, with thick glasses and a thicker beard, stepped into the hallway. He held a shotgun at his hip.

"Whoa, um," Grant said as he stumbled backward, his hands

in the air.

A woman and two young children came into view behind the homeowner. The children were smiling, as they didn't know any better. The woman's eyes were wide and she clutched her children like they'd be stolen away at any moment.

"Go back to the den!" the man yelled at them. By the way he said the words, Ian could tell the man was normally gentle with his family, but he sensed danger and wanted to protect them. His family hurried back in the direction from which they came.

"I'm sorry, sir," Ian said from behind Grant. "The dead are everywhere and this was the only place that seemed safe."

"As you can see," he lifted the gun, "I'm trying to keep it that way."

"You should have locked your door," Grant said. He didn't mean for it to sound like a threat, it really wasn't, but it did. The man cocked the gun. Grant stepped back again until he was almost on top of Ian, who was already up against the closed front door.

"You think you can walk into any house you want? Just because the world ended doesn't mean that everybody else went with it."

Ian wanted to calm the man enough for them to make it back outside without bullet holes in their bodies. "You are right. It was wrong of us." He reached behind himself for the doorknob and slowly turned it.

"Find another house!" the man seethed through gritted teeth. He didn't like playing the bad guy and his jaw was getting tired from clenching.

"Aye aye, captain!" Grant said, turning on his heels and running through the now open front door.

Outside, the street was full of the dead.

Ian glanced around for anything in which to hide, but the options were limited to some large dumpsters, with a stinky sludge in the bottom, and a child's small playhouse in the backyard next door.

Grant thought of a better idea.

"We can hide in the basement."

"Of *this* guy's house? No way!" Ian turned his back to Grant and considered the garbage cans again. *Sludge or shotgun?*

"They aren't using it and they'll never know we are there." Grant was already at the wooden door. It, like the front door, wasn't locked. They climbed in.

The basement was full of stuff. Furniture, paintings, stacks of books, and clothing that looked to date back to the fifties. There was a thin layer of moisture on the floor and the entire space smelled of mold. Grant led the way on a small path carved through the junk. The only place they could find to sit was near an old utility sink in the darkest corner. They sat shoulder to shoulder with their backpacks in front of them. Ian shone his flashlight and discovered piles of rat feces beneath the sink.

• • •

You've been in far worse places than this closet.

"But Grant was with me. He made things bearable."

• • •

Grant turned to humor to weather the situation. "Don't fart," he said.

"Don't make me laugh!" Ian hissed. He shifted his focus to other things, like the spider resting on its perfectly spun web above the sink. Several insects sat motionless on the sticky surface, waiting patiently to be devoured. Or maybe they were dead. Ian felt kinship with them. He knew what it was like to lay below the top of the food chain; to be stuck in impossible situations with, barring a miracle, little hope for survival.

Above them, they could hear the man pacing and yelling at his wife. The children began to scream. Breaking glass next and then the firing of the shotgun followed by the thump of a newly made corpse hitting the floor.

Now only one child screamed. The back door was thrown open and small feet made their way quickly down the back stairs.

Ian and Grant were both holding their breath and silently hoping no one would try to hide in the basement. They waited ten minutes before speaking.

"We led the dead right to them. We got them killed!" Ian was still watching the spider, which had begun to wrap its prey in small bundles of silk.

Grant shrugged. "The guy was a prick anyway."

"What about the kids? Don't you feel bad for them?"

"We're kids too, you know? I'm feeling pretty damaged right now."

"You've been damaged since birth, Grant."

"And now I'm hurting even more!"

Ian knew he was joking again. Grant wasn't serious about much of anything.

"How long are we going to stay here?" Grant asked. "My legs are cramping."

"You're the one who chose this bat cave so don't even start complaining. We have to wait even longer now. The screaming and the shotgun blasts didn't help our situation."

Grant stood up to move his legs and take a peek at the backyard. "Shit, it's like a party out there."

"We'll wait a bit longer and then go upstairs. Maybe we can make a run for it through the front yard."

• • •

A half hour later, the spider had eaten all the bugs in its web and Grant was growing impatient. Every so often, something moved upstairs.

"I think enough time has passed. Can we go up now?"

Ian looked through the basement's small windows. Outside, the sun was setting. "Yeah, we can't wait any longer."

The boys climbed the short set of stairs that led to the first floor of the house. They listened at the door. A soft dragging noise moved by on the other side.

"Should we check the kitchen for some food while we're here?" Grant asked, but his tone suggested it was merely to ask. He didn't want to stick around in a house of potentially swarming with zombies.

"Where's the front door from here?" Ian asked, ignoring Grant's question and answering it at the same time.

Grant closed his eyes and tried to remember the layout of the house. "Turn left and take the first right."

"I can't do it," Ian said. "I'm too scared to open the door."

Grant reached for the knob and threw the door open into the hallway. "Run!" he whispered.

Ian held his hands out in front of him, hoping they wouldn't touch anything unfriendly. The front door was open and the yard beyond it, clear.

"Into the first house without blood on it!" Grant yelled. "I'm right behind you."

• • •

This one was the only option.

"A place I never would have had to choose, except that..."

...I LET DOWN MY GUARD

Before the debacle in the neighborhood, Ian and Grant had plenty of food in their packs, but they stopped at a high school for Ian to quickly retie his shoes. Movement out of the corner of Grant's eye made them stay a moment longer.

"Whoa," Grant said. There, on the athletic field, three girls jogged around the track like it wasn't the end of the world. The boys watched their toned bodies move and their happy ponytails— and other things—bounce up and down. "We can't leave yet."

One of the girls noticed the boys. She pointed him out to her friends.

"Hey," one of them said breathlessly after running from the far end of the field. The other two came up beside her, equally winded.

"Um, hi?" Ian said, confused. It was such a normal, casual greeting. None of them were even armed.

"I'm Nikki, this is Elyse," the first girl said pointing to the brunette to her left, "and this is Cathleen. Like, who are you guys?" She flipped her hair.

Grant and Ian hated the valley girl type. It was a disappointment and Grant immediately changed his attitude. "Like, I'm Grant," he said, flipping long imaginary locks, mocking Nikki's mannerisms.

All three girls rolled their eyes. Nikki began to turn away from them and made to grab her friends' arms. Grant might not have cared, but Ian didn't want them to leave yet.

"That's a really good idea, staying in shape in case you have to fight," Ian said, trying to appeal to their egos. "You look like you would win."

"We aren't going to fight," Elyse scoffed. "We have to stay in shape or we won't fit in our uniforms." She bent at her waist and reached her hands to the ground in a stretch.

"Yeah," Cathleen chimed in. "Five pounds gained and it's muffin top central in my skirt."

"Wait, you were cheerleaders?" Grant asked. "Like 'rah rah' and all that?"

"We are *still* cheerleaders," Nikki corrected him. "And when school starts up again, so will the games."

"And we'll be ready!" Elyse said with so much joy on her face that it made Ian want to cry.

"School isn't going to start again," he said. "You should be thinking about the future. How are you going to survive?"

"We're doing fine, thank you!" Nikki spat before stomping toward a door on the side of the school.

The trio of girls wasn't the first group Ian and Grant had met that thought the world would quickly return to business as usual, but they still seemed more normal than the others.

"We should go inside," Cathleen said. "The creeps are starting to come around."

Ian examined the fences. "It's only a couple of zombies."

"Don't say the Z word!" Elyse shrieked. "Nikki hates it."

"Seems like she hates a lot of things." Grant shifted his backpack, which had begun to chafe his shoulders.

"Come on." Cathleen waved for them to follow her. "You can relax in the gym."

The gymnasium was hardly relaxing with its cold air and hardwood floors, but with few windows and only a couple of exits, it felt much safer than most places in which Grant and Ian had been. Nikki sat in a corner, removing her shoes, stretching, and then reading a book. Cathleen and Elyse disappeared into a side room and came out a short time later dragging a blue gym mat. Unfolded, it was large enough for five people to lie on.

"Your sleeping bags won't be very comfortable on just the floor. This should help!" Cathleen smiled and then jogged over to Nikki.

"We can stay?" Ian asked. They didn't seem eager for company, especially Nikki.

"For a night," Elyse answered. "I don't think Nikki wants you here longer than that."

• • •

You should have left then.

"How were we to know?"

Ian tries to remember any small detail that might have tipped him off to the things to come, but he still can't see anything suspicious in their actions.

Things too good to be true in the apocalypse usually are.

"Well you, my conscience, were asleep on the job."

Fair enough.

"Besides, they gave us food!"

• • •

"From the vending machines," Elyse said as she dropped an assortment of small plastic packages onto the mat. "Take whatever you want."

Cathleen dropped another armful on top of the rest. "Yeah," she said, "there's no way we need all of this. We have to watch our figures."

Grant and Ian considered the pile of junk food. They'd learned their lesson long before about eating crap. Grant chose a single Snickers bar and tucked it into a pocket of his backpack.

"Wow, that's really nice of you," Ian said, but he made no selections from the heap. Instead, he opened the top of his backpack and showed the girls its content. "And I'm not trying to be ungrateful, but we have everything we need. You should keep it."

Cathleen and Elyse rolled their eyes at one another.

"Whatever," Cathleen said.

"So, where are you three sleeping?" Grant asked. His question sounded sleazy, like he wanted to catch them in their underwear.

• • •

"He might not have liked cheerleaders, but girls were girls to

47

Grant. He definitely would have wanted to see them in any form of undress that they'd allow.

What about you?

"You know I'm pickier."

• • •

Elyse began to answer, but Nikki, who had come over stopped her. Her eyes were calling Grant "dirty" and "disgusting".

"That," Nikki said, "is none of your business!"

At dusk, the girls disappeared to another area of the school and Grant and Ian unpacked their sleeping bags. The blue mats added a surprising amount of warmth that night, allowing them to sleep more soundly than they had in weeks. When Ian awoke the next morning, he couldn't immediately tell that anything was wrong. It was only when he went to his backpack for breakfast that he found it to be empty. Grant's had been mostly emptied as well, except for a can of pinto beans. Even the Snickers bar was gone. He shook his friend awake and held his bag upside down near his face.

"They took nearly everything."

Grant sat up. "We've been fucking robbed by cheerleaders?" His voice echoed in the large gym. He slid out of his sleeping bag, stuffed it in his backpack and ran for the doors. "Keep up, Ian!"

"No wonder they gave us all the food. They were just going to take it right back anyway." Ian said as he followed. "We should be happy they didn't kill us because they could have."

"*They* should be hoping I don't kill *them*!" Grant threw open doors to classrooms and supply closets looking for the girls. The cafeteria was full of garbage; the staff lounge held piles of dirty clothes, and the bathrooms stunk of girl shit, which, in Grant's opinion, stunk worse than boys'. They found traces of the trio all over the school's campus, but no girls.

Ian sat on a bench in the courtyard to catch his breath. He didn't want to find them because seeing Grant hit a girl wasn't something that Ian thought he could un-see.

"Fuck! Fuck, fuck, fuck!" Grant screamed. "Where are they

hiding?"

"Maybe they've left?" Ian wished Grant would drop it. They'd lost supplies before when Ian's house burned down. It wasn't completely impossible to find more.

"Would you leave this setup? No way! As soon as we leave, they'll be back. The school is their home." He paced the length of the courtyard.

A lone zombie wandered into the area. Ian stood up slowly and walked to Grant, placing a hand on his shoulder to get his attention quietly. "Let's get out of here."

"Where the hell are we supposed to go? And where will we get more food?"

"We could go back to the grocery store or maybe get some from the houses. Anywhere. But there's nothing left here for us."

Ian hoped to leave the school behind for more reasons than the thieving girls and the shuffler in the courtyard. He wanted to distance himself from something painful that was scratching at a shipping container a few blocks behind them.

• • •

It's time to tell them about Ripley.

"I'm not ready to talk about her. I'll never be ready."

You told them about Grant, how you screwed up his life. Ripley made her own mistakes. It should be easy to talk about her.

"She was my first..." Ian says, remembering the closeness he shared with her. He inhales thinking he can smell her skin, but instead gets a noseful of the rotting bodies downstairs.

Welcome back to reality. Now tell them what you saw.

"My stint in the closet isn't the first time I've been without Grant and the dead girl downstairs and the cheerleaders aren't the first to have hurt me because..."

Michelle Kilmer

...I WENT AFTER RIPLEY

In a hostile world, beauty stands out; like flowers growing through cracks in the pavement or the fluid rainbow arcs in an oil slick. Ripley, the girl who wore a smile on her face as she dodged zombies in the street, was that beauty to Ian. She was an unforgettable brightness in the ever-darkening landscape.

On their journey east, the boys saw her looting a hardware store. Her work was quiet and meticulous. She was tall and lean and she appeared to be surviving much better than they were. Ian and Grant both stared at her like they hadn't seen a girl before. She glanced up and Ian waved to her with a grin on his face. She waved back. A motion so simple and normal, Ian couldn't get over it. Something about the return of such a silly gesture made him decide he needed to know the girl as much as she would let him.

He had lusted after many of the female species, but this was different. *Is this what love feels like?* He wondered.

"Let's not go too far before we find somewhere to stay for the night," Ian said to Grant. He didn't want to lose track of the beautiful girl and the farther they traveled away from her, the more zombies he'd have to get through to get back to her. He hoped it wasn't too obvious to Grant what his motives were.

"This place looks okay." Grant was referring to a sprawling bungalow with a low fence and a thick garden, dead from the winter. There wasn't a car in the driveway and the house was undisturbed by the chaos.

"Yeah, it does." Ian suppressed his enthusiasm.

"Hey, man. I saw you checking out that girl. I don't blame you. She was hot. I'd like to hole up with her somewhere."

Ian smacked Grant's shoulder. "Don't talk about her like that."

"Come on, Ian. We don't have time for relationships."

Ian was familiar with that tactic of Grant's. He'd used it before to keep another girl for himself. As soon as he turned his back, Grant would be outside trying to find what Ian wanted.

"She's mine. I saw her first." Ian tried to sound confident, dominant.

"Oh, I get it. The virgin boy wants a shot with a lady." Grant nudged his arm and winked exaggeratedly. "She does look easy, so I'm sure it's a possibility."

"Don't call me a virgin boy!" Ian thought it was only fair that he have a chance with the girl. Grant had already lost his virginity. It was Ian's turn. "Can you just be my wingman for once?"

"I doubt she'll say yes, but I won't stop you."

• • •

You didn't trust him.

"Hell no. Grant always got the girl. Between the two of us, they'd always choose him."

You don't sound too sour about it.

"Ha! I just couldn't give him the chance again."

So you snuck out.

• • •

They were sleeping in a bedroom that was centered in the house. It felt safe. That night, when Grant fell asleep, Ian left to find the girl. The floorboards moaned, but the sounds only blended into the nightscape.

Ian caught a glimpse of himself in a hallway mirror. He was surprised to find it a handsome reflection. Due to poor nutrition and quite a bit more exercise, Ian had lost weight and he was closing in on Grant's handsomeness. This bolstered his confidence and he strode out the front door as though it was a normal day and he was on his way to school.

But to step outside in the dark was a huge and unnecessary risk. It was akin to putting one foot in the grave. Every corner Ian turned held a new opportunity to die. Broken glass, starving stray dogs, and of course, zombies were just a few of the dangers he would encounter.

He walked carefully in the dark to where he thought she was living; a stack of cargo containers on one end of a construction area. The place was once surrounded by chain link fence, but it was pushed over in sections and the dead roamed in and out freely. He walked over one of the fallen fences and it crunched beneath his feet. In the dead world, even such a small noise was going to draw attention. Like clockwork, eight zombies turned in his direction.

In the middle of the lot was a large pit, several stories deep. Some of the infected, who had failed to avoid it, dragged themselves around its bottom. Ian circled around the hole several times, trying to lose zombies to the hole. Only four of them ended up falling, but four was enough to take the pressure off.

To reach the cargo containers, Ian had to walk by two portable offices. He was tempted to loot them, but the urge to see the girl was stronger so he continued on. A faint glow of candlelight reached through a crack in one of the metal boxes. He climbed the side, holding onto the grooves like rungs of a ladder, and pulled his way to the top. *Had any boy before me gone to such lengths to be with a girl?*

• • •

Your hormonal drive isn't unique.
"It's more unique now. Less competition if you haven't noticed."

• • •

His footsteps sent echoes into the container beneath him. The door, the one the candlelight was flickering behind, opened and the girl stepped out onto the makeshift balcony.

"Who's there?" she called out, throwing the beam of a flashlight in all directions trying to find the human source of the noise. Ian's heart leapt at the sound of her voice. It was sweeter than he imagined it would be.

He stepped into light, shielding his eyes from the intense scrutiny of the beam. "My name's Ian. I saw you earlier. You waved."

"Oh, you," she said. There was no detectable enthusiasm in

53

her voice, but she still took his hand and led him into the cold rectangle that was her home. Inside a single candle flickered. An older woman sat near it, rocking and mumbling to herself. Ian jumped, as he wasn't expecting that someone else would be inside the container. "Who's that?" he asked.

"My mother," the girl replied. She clicked off her flashlight and lit another candle next to the first.

Ian kept his eyes on the woman in case she might glance up and greet him, but she never did. "What's wrong with her? I mean...what happened?"

"It's okay. She saw my dad die. She was normal before that." She went to her mother's side and ran a hand over her head comfortingly. The woman's rocking slowed and her mumbling ceased.

"Were you there?" Ian asked. He couldn't imagine what it would be like to see a parent killed. Thankfully he was spared witnessing his mother's final moments.

"No. I was at school when it happened. My name's Ripley, by the way."

"Ripley?" Ian asked. *What a unique name*, he thought.

"My dad, he liked the movie *Alien*," she explained.

"It's a last name," Ian said, displaying his knowledge of the film. "In the movie, Ripley is her last name."

"Yeah I know." She shrugged. "I guess my dad didn't care."

She must hear that all the time. Shut up! Ian thought. *Change the subject!* "Why are you here? Why didn't you stay home?" he asked. A pile of clothes and bags was dumped by one wall, another area functioned as a makeshift kitchen.

"I thought somewhere else might be safer than our house and my dad is still there, you know, walking around."

• • •

You know exactly what it's like to avoid bodies.
"I guess I should be thankful that the ones I'm avoiding aren't walking around anymore."
You put an end to that.

54

Images storm Ian's mind. He can see the chair leg in his hands, the moment of first impact with Grant's head, and the blood on his hands when it was over.

"I don't want to see these things!" Ian yells.

Come back to Ripley's story then. What did you say next?

• • •

"Nowhere is really safe." Ian scanned the room for weapons. He saw a small fixed-blade knife, a hockey stick with blood on its toe, but nothing else even remotely dangerous or protective. Perhaps the flashlight could be used in a bludgeoning.

"I had to pick this place, up high, and stock up like crazy, because of my mom. She screams sometimes and it brings the dead. I lock her in when I leave. The food, out. I can't trust her. I wish she had died with him because I know I could survive on my own; it's taking care of her that's the difficult part."

• • •

You didn't show it, but you were shocked to hear that from her.

"Yes, she still had her mom. She should have been thankful."

The grass is always greener, isn't it?

"I'd give a lot to have my mom back. I'd even take one of my dad's lectures on 'unhealthy behavior.' I could really fucking use that right now."

At least you still had Grant. You told her about him, didn't you?

• • •

"Grant, the guy with me earlier, he and I take care of each other like brothers. I've known him since I was little."

"That's nice. I never had anyone like that. Isn't he going to wonder where you are?"

"He was asleep when I left, but if he were to wake up I think he'd know where I went." Ian hoped it didn't sound dirty, like all guys think about is bedding the ladies. Which was kind of true, but she didn't need to know it.

She seemed to have the same thing on her mind though for she said, "Before we...do anything, I have to feed my mom."

Ian's mom had fed others at the hospital. It was messy

and took patience and sometimes the patients didn't want to eat. Sometimes, they became violent. Often, more of the food ended up on her or on the floor. "Do you actually have to feed her?"

"No, she can still do that, but I have to prepare the food. I'm the chef." Ripley dug through a box and pulled out a can of chowder and a very old baguette. It had a few spots of mold on the crust that she carefully cut away. When she was done, Ian took the bread from her and hit it on the card table. It was in the last stage of stale: rock solid.

"You could kill a man with this," he joked, trying to lighten the situation.

She grabbed it back. "Not if you dip it in the soup first. It softens." She lit the flame of a small camp stove and dumped the chunky chowder into a pot. Once the chowder was warmed, she poured a single bowl and set it down on the floor in front of her mother. She set the baguette next to it and kissed her mother's forehead.

"Do you want anything to eat?" Ripley asked.

Ian shook his head. The last thing he needed before losing his virginity was a belly full of sloshing soup. His stomach was churning anyway, from a mix of excitement and nervousness.

Ripley grabbed his hand and led him to her bedroom, which was nothing more than a bed and an overturned crate as a table. A sheet hung from the ceiling of the shipping container and acted as a wall. They lay down on her bed, which was only a pile of flattened cardboard covered with a sheet and quilt. She cuddled close to him.

Ian's heart began to pound and he could feel his cheeks and his crotch growing warm.

"I'm sorry if I smell," she said self-consciously. "I haven't bathed in a few days."

"I'm sure I smell far worse. I've been running around a lot."

"Yeah and you're a *boy*," she said through a laugh.

"A boy who forgot to pack his deodorant."

"You know, there's a 'take one, get one free' sale at every

store in town right now. It wouldn't be much trouble for you to get some."

She's cute and funny, he thought. *How did I get so lucky?*

Ian was quickly running out of things to talk about. His life revolved around Grant and survival, and Grant was the last thing he wanted to bring up. He touched the thin fabric wall that separated them from Ripley's mother.

"It's a little weird, you know, with your mom out there," Ian said. He worried she would become bored of her meal, wander over, and snap out of her senility long enough to chew him out for banging her daughter.

"She doesn't pay attention anymore," Ripley replied as she blew out a candle, the only light source.

"This is my first time," Ian finally admitted to her in the dark. His hands felt heavy and awkward, but Ripley began to guide them and his nerves calmed. She was obviously not a virgin. There was something primitive about the low bed, the dirt of the construction site, and the metal smell from the container walls. Ian felt an animalistic energy come over him as he entered her. Ripley moaned softly and then covered her own mouth with a hand to stifle the noise.

After they finished, they lay next to each other in the dark. Now that Ian was no longer a virgin, he was suddenly less shy and couldn't stop touching her skin. It was soft and warm, made softer and warmer by the juxtaposition of their industrial surroundings. Ian was beginning to fall asleep when a dry and wretched noise came from the "living room" area. "What is that?"

Ripley sighed. "My mother. I'll go check on her." She reached for a flashlight and turned it on. Ian got a quick peek of her naked body before she pulled on her dirty clothes. Ripley dragged her feet as she went to her mother's aid.

"Oh my god! She's choking! Help me!" she called out to Ian.

Ian felt around for his own clothes, dressed, and ran to them. Ripley pushed the flashlight to his chest. "Hold this!" she yelled.

He held it above the woman's face with a trembling hand

as she struggled for breath. Ripley plunged a finger down her mother's throat in an attempt to free the piece of bread, but she only succeeded in lodging it further down.

"Dammit! Hold the light over her mouth!" she screamed. Ian had closed his eyes from exhaustion, but also to keep from seeing the woman as she was dying and that caused the beam of light to move to an area on the side of her head near her right ear. At some point the woman stopped breathing and her face lost its last spots of color, but still Ripley tried to dislodge the bread.

Ian put a hand to Ripley's shoulder. "She's gone. It won't help. We need to get out of here," he warned her, but she was in a daze. Her mother's eyes were empty, but open. Ian knew it was time to go when he saw them move once again.

"Ripley!" Ian said forcefully. At that moment, as her name crossed his lips, her mother's mouth closed on the fingers that were still inside of it. Ripley screamed and yanked until her hand was released. She stared down at the bleeding stumps of three missing fingers.

• • •

"I should have pulled her hand out."

At least you used your voice that time. You couldn't do as much for Grant.

"I could have saved her and let her mother die! And she could have come to live with us and then maybe I never would have let Lena in! Maybe we would have found a better house!"

Watch your volume. You'll alert the beasties.

"She fucking thought she was going to be fine!"

• • •

"It's okay. I just n-n-n-need to sto-p-p-p-p the bleeding," Ripley stuttered, still unable to take her eyes off of the space where her fingers used to be.

Ian backed away. "You know that won't help." He moved away slowly because he didn't want to seem like a complete jerk. The wound, though technically non-fatal if treated quickly, would kill her. If the blood loss didn't end her life, her infected mother's saliva would. It was toxic and already mixing with her blood, traveling through her veins. She would die.

She would come back.

Ripley was in shock and Ian used that to his advantage. He knew he had overstayed his welcome. He closed the shipping container's door and locked her inside as she had her mother. But he couldn't yet leave. Her screams from inside where attracting a new group of zombies to the foot of the container tower.

"Ian! Please open the door! "

"You know why I can't, Ripley! I'm sorry!" He yelled back through the metal door. "I'm sorry." He listened to her pound on it. Each thwack sent daggers through his heart. Each tearful cry, growing quieter as she weakened, burned his ears.

"My mom. She's getting-" Her final words.

Ian heard a soft thud as Ripley's body hit the floor. Blood was seeping out from under the door; too much blood. Her death had come.

He waited for a while longer in the new silence. The dead below began to disperse. Before he climbed down, he heard two sets of dragging feet carrying lifeless bodies around the small and cluttered interior of the shipping container.

• • •

She stayed with her mother in death as she had in life.

"I had a chance to free her."

There was no way to know what would become of them.

• • •

Tears fell from Ian's eyes as he walked back to the bungalow. He walked slowly and carelessly, unconcerned if he lived or died. Ian's reflection in the mirror had changed. He was more mature and defeated at the same time. Grant was still sleeping.

• • •

And Grant never knew.

"No, he didn't even know that I snuck out that night."

But you wanted to tell him.

"I wanted to brag, but I couldn't think of Ripley without seeing blood."

You still can't.
"Will I ever?"
Grant didn't let you brag much. He knew you were a wimp. Tell them about the guns. Maybe if you had had one, you could have saved her.

...I WASN'T TRIGGER HAPPY

It was one thing to shoot guns in video games and have discussions with your best friend about recoil and stopping power, it was a completely different thing to hold a gun in your hand and take a life. Ian had been purposely avoiding it and, through luck alone, a usable weapon hadn't presented itself.

Now, with the Discount Gun Shop dead ahead and Grant's eyes already dreaming of the haul that awaited them inside, Ian knew he'd be holding one within the hour. And when the inevitable happened, he'd have to pretend that it didn't scare the hell out of him.

• • •

You're really frightened by a lot of things.
As soon as his brain thinks the word 'frightened', it goes crazy with imagery.
"I wouldn't say a lot," Ian lies.
You can't fool me. I see what you see. Long-legged spiders, plane crashes, being alone.
"That's why you're here. If I keep talking to you, I'll never be alone."
Or you'll always be...

• • •

The front door was unlocked. Ian pushed it gently, in case a warning bell triggered or a zombie was just inside. Grant slid through the opening and into the darkness of the shop and Ian followed. They both procured flashlights from their backpacks and shone them on the walls. The pegboards were empty, the display cases too. There wasn't one single gun in sight.

"Looks like they sold out a long time ago," Ian said. He tried to hide his relief. There weren't any boxes of bullets that he could see either.

"Dammit!" Grant yelled. He wanted a gun desperately. It was the only weapon that would make him feel safe. His nose caught a strange scent. "What's that smell?" he asked.

Ian sniffed the air. "Paint, I think." He walked slowly behind the counter and into a large storage room. The beam of his flashlight found the source of the smell. "Yeah, it's paint."

Grant came to stand beside Ian. "Fucking hell!" he screamed.

A large pile of guns, the store's entire non-looted selection, was sitting in the middle of the floor covered in pink paint. Emptied paint cans littered the perimeter of the pile.

"Every last one of them is fucking useless!" Grant whined. "We don't have time to figure out how to clean them."

Though the smell was strong and the expression on Grant's face was pitiful, Ian said a silent *thank you* to whoever had damaged the merchandise. "Someone took what they wanted and made sure no one else had the opportunity."

Grant picked up a handgun from the pile, some of the paint on it was still wet. "Who the fuck would do something like this?" he asked, though he had an idea.

Ian searched the storeroom for the answer and he found it. There, on the door, was a sloppily scrawled set of initials in the same bright pink paint that covered the guns.

"KK," Ian said. "Keller did this."

Grant dropped the gun and it sent paint splattering outwards from its landing spot. "And the award for asshole of the century goes to…"

"Well, nothing's really useful here so maybe we should keep moving."

"Can't you at least pretend to be sad?" Grant knew Ian was uneasy around firearms. The first time they'd played a shooting game on his Xbox, Ian flinched every time he pulled the trigger. "One of these days you'll have no choice but to fight. Whether the weapon in your hand is a gun or not, well, who knows? But you need to get over this shit. We aren't kids anymore."

• • •

And yet you still made the other choice.
"I should have dug through the guns with him. I should have found something useful.
There had to have been something, but Grant couldn't find it through his anger.
"I could have, but I just didn't want to."
The girls at the high school might not have messed with you if you had.
"Guns do more bad things than good."
Like with Markie.
"Yes, like with him."

Michelle Kilmer

...I DIDN'T SAVE MARKIE

Where would you go when the world ends? What places would you avoid? When Grant and Ian saw the Quality Food Center and its parking lot, which had been blocked off by vehicles, it had all the markings of a great place to ride out the apocalypse: few entrances, plenty of food, and loads of open space surrounding it for nothing to take them by surprise. The only thing that kept them from breaking the perimeter was the four or five men that patrolled it; big, bearded men with guns and attitude. They looked frighteningly organized and ready to kill without warning.

Still, the lure of a safe place kept Ian and Grant lurking on the perimeter.

A teenager climbed out of the encampment, over the bed of a pickup truck and straight toward them in the woods. As he got closer, Ian recognized him as another friend of Grant's.

"Markie!" Grant whispered.

Ian nodded in acknowledgment. He hadn't talked to Markie much at school, but the two boys knew of one another.

"Hey, man! Shit!" Markie had a special handshake that he did with all of his friends and he and Grant performed the short collection of slaps, fist bumps, and shakes. "What are you guys doing out here?"

"Scoping out a place to stay. You?"

"Comin' out to piss."

Ian looked longingly at the store, of which he could only see the roof. The ring of vehicles was effective in keeping the dead out.

"You'd be safer if you rolled with us," Markie said. He lifted his shirt to show a gold-plated gun tucked into his waistband.

"We don't need guns to stay safe from the dead, Markie,"

Ian said. The gun made him nervous. Markie with a gun made him even more nervous.

"You might not need protection from them, but Rachel can give you a lot."

"Who's Rachel?"

"She's the baddest bitch you've ever seen and if you defy her, well, you die."

"Why would we want to come inside then?" Ian asked. They'd just been kicked out of a drug store and they needed an easy place to stay, but this didn't sound like it. It sounded like a repeat of the hell they'd just left. Same troubles, different players.

"You can come in, but only if you plan on staying for a long time. Rachel doesn't take kindly to folks who just want to pass through. She has some weird ideas."

"Like what?"

"She likes the chaos, the zombies. She's happy the world has changed."

"That *is* weird," Ian said. He put extra emphasis on his reaction in the hope that Grant wouldn't drag him inside of the death trap.

Luckily, Grant was already pulling Ian away by his backpack. "I think we'll pass."

Markie nodded. "Don't say I didn't try to help you out!" He shrugged and ran back to the store.

"Quit tugging on my bag!" Ian ripped free of Grant's grasp. "What the hell?"

"You've heard the rumors. His dad is in a gang. I don't want to get mixed up in that shit."

"You don't have to convince me. I think we should stay solo for awhile."

• • •

"Funny how Grant led us into the motorcycle gang's lair, but this was different."

He knew the guys in the motorcycle club. It was absolutely different.

"They were guilty of just as many crimes and killings."

Mistakes I Made During the Zombie Apocalypse

You're on trial here. Not them! Not Grant!

• • •

The boys were preparing to move on, as the day was turning to night, when they saw a woman exit the grocery store.

"That must be Rachel," Ian said.

"She's hot," Grant observed. "Got that resting bitch face though."

"Who's that guy?" Ian asked. A man dressed in dark clothing and armed with guns and a blade was sneaking around the outskirts of the parking lot. He watched Rachel and the other men. Ian and Grant watched him take out all of the tires of the vehicle barrier with his knife.

"He's serious, whoever he is."

"We should leave. *Now.*"

"Stay quiet. This could benefit us."

Ian was about to ask how, but then he realized a war between second and third parties might leave them the spoils.

They lay as low as possible as a gunfight broke out and even when the fight moved into the store, the boys held back.

More gunfire and then three people excited the store; Rachel, the armed man, and a tall blonde who looked like a Viking. Then, a grenade went off, taking the Viking with it.

After the explosion, and after the man who'd caused the fight collected the guns and left, the boys approached the store. Small fires burned in the lot, pieces of the larger man's body hung on everything. Near the door, they came upon a smoldering corpse of a woman. Grant wanted to linger and take in the carnage, but Ian pulled him inside the store.

There, between two of the registers, they found Markie and a man Grant recognized as Markie's father. A bullet to the brain had killed the older man as he held his son's body. Markie had bled out from a stab wound and returned to life. His father's embrace was too tight though, keeping Markie from roaming the aisles. He struggled to break free as a meal hovered over him.

Grant lifted the knife, wiped it on Markie's pants, and tucked it into his own belt. "Shit," he said, trying to avoid the biting mouth of his old friend. "His dad always watched over him. He must have been pretty broken up when he died."

"Should we do something?" Ian asked.

"You mean, kill him?" Grant then saw the golden gun, discarded beneath the register counter. He checked the magazine. "There are a couple bullets left. Do you want to do it?"

Here it was, the opportunity Ian was hoping to avoid. He'd never killed anyone, living or undead. The golden gun, with a light smattering of blood from Markie's father's head on its muzzle, was held out to him. He couldn't take it or a *life*.

"I can't watch." He backed away as Grant took no time in aiming at Markie's forehead.

"A gun with one bullet isn't much use," Grant said before dropping it to the floor.

• • •

Is this really a mistake, not saving Markie?
"He wasn't a bad kid."
You hardly knew him. I think you should let go of it.
"Maybe you're right. I'm carrying enough as it is."
Now we're making some progress!

• • •

"There isn't a lot room in my pack," Grant said as they perused the shelves for foodstuff. It was a good problem to have, but a problem nonetheless.

"We could swap some stuff out," Ian suggested. "Get rid of some of the gross things that Thomas gave us."

"You mean the canned artichokes, don't you?" Grant knew just what pocket the can of slimy vegetable was in and he fished it out. A can of chili filled its place in the pack.

"What about these crackers?" Ian held up a partially collapsed box of Saltines.

Grant shook his head. "We're not having a repeat of the communion wafers. They'll dry out your mouth!"

"Is your advice in the apocalypse to pick wet stuff?" Ian

laughed. Though the aisles were messy, the grocery store was a place of calm and near normalcy. It felt good to joke around.

"Yes, Ian. Pick wet stuff…like this can of pineapple slices."

• • •

"I almost felt like Edith was going to pop out and make us pay for everything we took."

Oh yes, Edith. A very special woman.

"We wouldn't have had to re-kill Markie if Edith hadn't kicked us out."

That was your fault.

"Yeah. It was."

Michelle Kilmer

...I BROKE THE RULES

The Walgreens presented itself as a promising looting opportunity. Whereas most of the storefronts had broken windows, its front windows were still intact. And though the specials advertised on the glass were outdated, Ian and Grant knew that the only numbers that mattered were the expiration dates printed on the cans and boxes inside. The one thing keeping them from entering through the front doors was the large "alive inside" spray-painted across the glass. The message should have kept them from entering at all. One should *never* make their presence known in the apocalypse! But they needed to eat and after what had happened with the bikers, they had to be cautious.

• • •

"I haven't told them about the bikers yet," Ian says with a hint of anger in his voice.
What happened with them directly affected your choices afterward. It's worth mentioning.
"Okay, but don't give anymore away. I'll tell their story next."
Whatever you say, boss. Back to Walgreens we go.

• • •

"If there really are people inside," Grant said to Ian, "we should go in through the back. They wouldn't be hanging out in the storage room, right?"

They tried the back door and surprisingly, it was unlocked. Cautiously, Grant led the way into the dark space. They made it halfway through when he ran into a stack of something set dead center in the middle of the floor. What sounded like empty cans clattered about the cement. Someone rushed into the room from within the store and shone a flashlight on them.

"Oh boys! Hello, hello, hello! Welcome, welcome, welcome!"

a person said in a high-pitched female voice. She grabbed them and pulled them through a set of swinging doors. In the light, they could see that she was a middle-aged woman with long, curly hair and big eyes. She was wearing a light blue polo shirt, a multi-colored floral apron, and neon green Crocs. A small clipboard, also neon green, dangled from a chain looped around a fanny pack strapped around her waist.

Now, there are a whole handful of people you shouldn't trust in the apocalypse: folks with more weapons than you, religious zealots, criminals, overly helpful individuals (they are always up to something), young children who have somehow managed to survive on their own and bubbly, wide-eyed housewives who don't seem to notice that the world is dying around them. Edith MacAllister's smile was so large Ian could see the woman's back molars and her eyes so brimming with enthusiasm they looked as though they might pop out of her head.

She picked up the clipboard and procured a pen from her fanny pack. "What are your names?" she asked. It seemed a bit formal, like the first day of school.

"Ian," Ian said and then he pointed to Grant, "Grant."

"Ian and Grant." She scrawled their names on the clipboard. I'm Edith MacAllister, but the family calls me Em."

"Your family is here?" Grant asked. Few people were lucky to hold onto their family during the destructive first days of the plague.

"No, well, you know, the others here with me. We were all shopping when people started getting sick outside."

"And you didn't try to get home? Don't you have a real family?" Ian asked. Grant hit him secretly. He could already tell that Edith was a little nuts.

"I'm sure they didn't make it. But enough about them! Tell me all about you two boys!"

"My parents are…gone," Ian said.

"And mine never gave a fuck," Grant said dryly.

Edith cringed. "Anyway, enough with the sad stuff." She

reached her hand into a pocket on the apron and removed two slips of paper. "You are welcome to stay, but you'll need to follow these rules."

Grant and Ian took the lists, but when Grant started into the store, Edith stopped him.

"I need you to read the rules and agree to them before you come in any further. You can sit in those chairs by the door. I hope you understand."

The rules weren't what Ian expected. He thought they'd be simple, like "No Pets" or "Wipe Your Feet", maybe "No Swearing". Instead, the paper laid out the strangest set of guidelines he'd ever read.

• • •

You still have the list don't you?
"I'm sitting on it." Ian pulls a folded piece of paper from his back pocket. "Here it is."
You don't even need to read it to remember what it says.
"Nope, they'll stay with me forever."

• • •

"Rule number one," Grant read, "No one is allowed in the toy aisle after 8pm."

"What's in the toy aisle after that?" Ian asked. "Gremlins?"

Grant laughed so hard he spit on his copy of the list. "Rule number two: Never open the reach-ins."

"That one isn't too bad." The milk appeared normal from where he was sitting, but he could imagine the spoiled smell of a dairy product left unrefrigerated for too long.

"Rule number three: All merchandise used or consumed must be documented for reimbursement to the company at a later date. Please use the back of this list. Additional paper can be purchased if needed."

"Whoa, what?"

"That's crazy."

Grant pulled on a strap of his backpack. "We'll use our own supplies first. I don't even have any money on me."

"Rule number four: No underage smoking, drinking or sex out of wedlock. This is still the real world."

"Ha! Who wrote these?" Ian asked.

"From the look on Edith's face when I said the 'eff' word, I'd guess she did."

• • •

"I could deal, but Grant especially didn't like the list."

Number four.

"Yeah. Grant smoked off and on since he was ten. He didn't like being told how to behave."

Sounds like someone else I know.

• • •

"So, if you agree to the rules, I'll introduce you to the others." Edith shifted her weight from one foot to the other, eager to begin introductions.

A quiet and clean place to sit was all either of the boys wanted. They nodded and followed her deeper into the store.

"This is the group!" Edith exclaimed as she gestured to four people sitting and standing around the aisles at the center of the drugstore. She offered no names to either party.

Three women and one man nodded lazily. Not out of disinterest for the boys, but seemingly out of annoyance with Edith's excitement over them.

"I'll let you all get acquainted. I have some business to attend to." She hurried off into an isolated corner of the store, down an aisle with the detergent and other cleaning chemicals.

"Does she maybe have a few screws loose?" Grant asked, directing his gaze at the one adult male, thinking he might be the most willing to share the dirt on "Em."

"She's addicted to smelling the detergents, especially the Tide. And sometimes she disappears down the Greeting Card aisle and cries over the sappiest ones."

"Why do you stay here with Em?" Ian asked.

"First," one of the women said, "We don't call her that. She *wants* us to call her that. And second, have you been outside? She might be a little nuts, but she isn't going to try to eat me."

"Wait until the food runs out," another of the women said, sending a hearty chuckle through the small group.

Grant was correct about the man, for he had more to spill on the wacky, self-appointed leader. "She took all the coupons out of the newspapers at the front. She thinks they'll honor them when things go back to normal. I believe she has a rewards card too. But she tracks it like everyone else. She had to get a new notepad 'cause she 'ran out of room.'"

"Coupons expire, you know," Ian pointed out.

"I guess common sense does too. Anyway, I'm Andy and this is Rosie, Brenda, and Jean. Pick an aisle, make yourselves at home."

• • •

The boys spent two peaceful days with the Walgreens survivors, playing Yahtzee the man had "purchased", tending to small blisters that had formed on their overworked feet with a first aid kit one of the women shared, and slowly and carefully dipping into their own food supplies, all while avoiding interacting with Edith if it could be helped. On the third day, however, Grant couldn't handle the monotony anymore. He pulled a copy of the last *Rolling Stone* magazine to be published from the rack. He thumbed through it and was putting it back when Edith came rushing down the aisle. It was though she sensed when the products on the shelves shifted.

"Did you add that to your list?" she asked, pointing at the publication.

"No, I don't want to keep it. I'm done with it."

"It doesn't work that way. This isn't a library. This is aisle 15 of the Northgate Walgreens. You've bent the pages; gotten your greasy fingerprints on the pictures. They won't be able to sell that to someone else when they reopen."

"You're kidding me, right?" He knew she wasn't. Her face was deadly serious, but it only made him want to mess with her more.

"Write it down, hand over some money, I don't care! But you

best not leave it on the shelf all used and dirtied. It's theft."

• • •

Ian's stomach growls loudly. It sounds like the hungry cry of one of the zombies. He turns over and lays his belly down on a fist.

Laying on it won't make it go away.

"What else am I supposed to do?" Ian asks himself.

You never dug through Grant's bag. He could have stashed something.

Ian quiets his mind and continues lying on his fist. Touching Grant's belongings seems like a bad idea to him. They are piled in the corner of the bedroom in a sort of shrine to his dead friend. There was no other way to honor him besides respecting his things.

Honor him by honoring the expiration date on the can of pinto beans in his backpack.

Ian jumps to his feet, opens the closet door and runs to the cairn of fabric and gear. He stands before it, but still cannot bring himself to touch anything.

You'll die, Ian. Grant wouldn't want you to die.

A sensation creeps over him, one of being watched. The feeling you get when someone else is in the room, like the airspace has shifted to allow their presence.

"He'll see me and he'll get pissed off that I touched his things."

There is no one here but you. Grant is dead, Ian. The beans are yours now.

Ian forces himself to turn around and face whatever demon stands behind him, but he only sees the partially opened bedroom door. He wraps himself in Grant's sleeping bag. The beans are slimy, bland, and cold, but Ian savors every mushy bite.

Remember what happened next in the great magazine debacle?

"Edith ate toothpaste." Ian laughs at the memory.

• • •

"How desperate are you for entertainment that you'd steal?" Edith yelled. She pulled a tube of toothpaste from the front pocket of her floral apron and began to nurse on the thing as though it was a Gogurt. Everyone could see she had several more tubes on standby for when she sucked the first one dry.

"You are eating *toothpaste*! If that isn't desperate, I don't know what is," Grant said.

"This isn't desperation! I'm on a budget and I had two-for-one coupons! Besides, the mint flavor calms me down."

Edith's refusal to loot during end times was annoying to say the least and her suggestion that she was capable of operating in a calm state of mind was comical to Grant.

"I don't think you know what the word 'calm' means, lady," he spat.

"Look you piece of shit," Edith screeched, "your mother may have let you disrespect her like this, but I won't stand for it!"

Ian wasn't prone to fits of rage or violence, but when he heard the word 'mother', it set him off and he took up Grant's fight as though it were his own. "No, *you* look you psycho bitch! My mother was great. You should be dead instead of her!"

Grant laughed.

The other Walgreens survivors gasped.

Edith's face went red. The tube of toothpaste dropped to the floor, sending a small glob of the mint-flavored dental hygiene goo shooting out onto Edith's Crocs. She opened her mouth to speak, but she could find no words. One of the women ushered her away, down the greeting card aisle, her sanctuary, where heavy sobs could be heard.

"I think you boys should leave," the man said.

"Fuck you and your stupid rules," Grant replied.

In the secluded back parking lot of the building, they sat on a curb to formulate a plan. Grant pulled open his backpack.

"I smuggled some stuff out." He presented Ian with a tube of ChapStick, a deck of cards, a travel-sized package of Q-Tips, and a book of crossword puzzles. It was an odd assortment, but Ian saw the usefulness of each item and wholeheartedly approved of Grant's rebellion.

• • •

The sun is going down outside the mostly abandoned house. Ian still sits in the bedroom, wrapped in Grant's sleeping bag, the empty bean can beside him. He goes to the window to study the world before the light disappears once again. A thick fog has come in and for a moment he pretends the world is normal beneath it.

A corpse, a thick man in a motorcycle jacket, breaks free of the white veil. "I know him," Ian says to himself. "I remember him from before Walgreens. From when…"

...I JOINED AN UNSKILLED ARMY

The zombies continued to pursue them, unconcerned for the boys' emotional well-being. They just had to keep on living; to survive and to survive hard.

If you didn't know what you were looking at, you might think the local motorcycle club's "clubhouse" was just another biker bar; a bar you never dreamed of setting foot in and most likely crossed the street to avoid walking in front of. But it was more than that. Even before the end of the world, with its few windows and secure entry, it was a stronghold that kept unwanted folks out and protected the membership from other gangs and public scrutiny. As an apocalypse bonus, zombies had a hell of a time breaching the fortress.

Grant and Ian stood on top of a pawnshop on the other side of the road, observing a row of twenty motorcycles parked in front of the bar. They couldn't stay an army of two any longer and the motorcycle club seemed to be a good answer.

"Look, I know the guys," Grant assured Ian. "My dad used to ride with them before he left. He intentionally withheld the part where his dad had been kicked out of the club for losing his *kutte*, or club vest, in a bar fight with a rival gang.

• • •

That was an important bit of information.
"He didn't know that."
I think he did. It would have saved a lot of trouble.
"Can I keep telling the story, please?" Ian asks the airspace.
Go right ahead.

• • •

A man—dressed in true biker getup: jeans, boots, and a leather jacket with a large 3-piece patch on the back—stepped outside of the club to smoke. His beard was a memorable shock of red hair.

"That's Big Jack," Grant said as they watched the man casually finish his cigarette while the dead closed in on him. "He's the president."

"So if we want to join up with them, he's the guy to talk to?" Ian was hoping for someone more approachable, not the six-foot-five bearded giant who clearly felt no fear.

"He's the *only* guy to talk to. If we ask anyone else, Big Jack will get mad."

The motorcycle club president flicked the butt of his cigarette at a zombie who'd made it within five feet of him, punched the walking corpse in the face, turned toward the door of the fortress, and went back inside.

"Yeah, let's not make him mad," Ian said.

The boys watched the small crowd of zombies build, tear at the brick facade of the club, and then give up when they could make no progress.

"Time to reintroduce myself," Grant said with a sigh.

"Here goes nothing," Ian said.

• • •

That would have been a good opportunity to walk the other way.

"I know, I know. But Grant insisted the club would help us."

• • •

Ian knocked on the door.

• • •

I thought you said no one knocks in the apocalypse.

"This was different. These guys were clearly dangerous. You're interrupting too much."

• • •

The dead turned on their heels when they heard the sound. Grant knocked next, louder and more insistent. Ian watched nervously as the reanimates moved closer. They were nearing the parked motorcycles and had begun to filter through them.

Come on, Ian thought. *Let us in.*

A thickly set man, who Grant later told Ian was nicknamed Tank, opened the club door.

"Whatcha want?" he asked gruffly.

Ian could hear the bikes being jostled back and forth behind them as the dead pushed through the makeshift barricade.

"Who is it?" Big Jack yelled as he came back to the front door.

"A couple boys," Tank replied as he moved aside to allow the club's president to see them both.

"Well, I'll be damned," Big Jack said with a grin. "You're Tony's kid."

"Grant," Grant reminded him with a slow nod, unsure that acknowledging the relation to his father was a good idea. "This is my friend Ian."

• • •

"I wasn't sure that I wanted to be 'Grant's friend' just then."
You were scared.

"I was terrified. These people were outlaws, criminals."
But not all of them remember? Tell them who else sought refuge with the bikers?

• • •

"Come on in, *kids*," Big Jack said, stressing the word 'kids' as if to remind the boys of their unequal status. "Make it quick, the zoms are getting through."

Hanging lamps brightly lit the inside of the club. A low hum of a generator could be heard burning fuel in the distance. A funk hung in the air and with each inhale Ian's nostrils registered another cause of the smell—old vomit, unwashed bodies, rotting drink garnishes, blood. The bar was fully stocked with empty bottles, drained early on by the club members. Generations of flies, from squirming maggots to adult flies flitting about, had made the bar's prep station their home. Food encrusted plates sat in an unrun dishwasher.

"Gross," Ian said quietly.

"Make yourselves at home, boys." Big Jack made no effort to

introduce the other men, all fifteen of them. The club president walked to a pool table and continued a game.

● ● ●

You aren't telling them who else was there.
"I'm getting there. Don't hype her up."
You're right. She isn't anything special.

● ● ●

They walked to an unoccupied table, set their bags down next to it and lowered into the dirty wooden chairs. At the back of the club, a door swung open.

A man and woman were laughing and showing certain public displays of affection that Ian had only see in online short films that he wasn't supposed to have watched. Her face was hidden as the man licked and kissed her exposed flesh. She wore a thin lace tank top, jean cutoffs, and cowboy boots.

"Hey, Colleen," Big Jack yelled from the pool table, "I thought you said he was dead."

The woman pushed the affectionate man off of her and stumbled closer to Ian and Grant.

"Mom?" Grant asked incredulously. "What the fuck?"

"Hey, baby," she slurred. "How ya' doing?" She sauntered over to Grant and held her arms out to him for a hug.

Grant's mother had hugged him few times in his life. He could remember all three. Once she did it in front of a social worker to keep him in her custody. Another time she awkwardly hugged him at the one parent-teacher meeting she'd attended in order to please the teacher about their "home life". The last time was when Grant's dad left them for good and she was high out of her mind, she didn't know what she was doing.

Grant chose to remain seated. "What are you doing here?" he asked.

"Spending some quality time with your dad's old friends," she answered. The man she'd been fooling around with smacked her butt playfully.

Grant knew what 'quality time' meant. It meant drugs,

drinking and sex. It meant not caring that your teenage son was unaccounted for. "You told them I was dead?"

"I figured, since I hadn't seen you around. Everybody else is dead. The neighbor lady, my dealer, you."

"No, mom! I'm not dead. I'm right here." He believed that she was dead as well. She survived on opiates, beer and a sporadic consumption of food, mostly the fast kind. She'd be better off dead.

"She's drunk, Grant." Ian didn't need to point it out. It was obvious. Colleen couldn't stand, think or speak well enough to be deserving of the title "adult".

"Ain't this little family reunion sweet!" Big Jack said mockingly. He was the type of man who found stolen bike parts, rival gang deaths and zombie face punching sweet, not families. "Too bad Tony couldn't be here."

"I heard he got the infection," Tank, one of the other bikers said from another of the dirty tables. When he spoke, he sounded like a child or at least a very dumb adult.

"No," Colleen replied, "he's in prison. He's safe there." She then sat down on the carpet as the alcoholic exhaustion hit her. None of the men moved to help her to a better seat.

"Ha, he's safe from zombies anyway. I know some guys in there who are after much more than yer brains," Big Jack said.

Laughter came spilling from the mouths of the many men in the room. Colleen giggled from the floor, though she was too drunk to actually understand the joke.

Grant leaned in toward Ian and whispered, "I can't stand to be around her. We should leave, find somewhere else."

"We have nowhere to go right now!" Ian whispered back. It wasn't like him to be so insensitive to his friend, but the bar was safer than any other place they'd found yet. "Find a way to ignore her, like you always have."

"Ahem," Big Jack—who'd once again stopped his pool game and come back to the main bar room—pretended to clear his throat. "This is my clubhouse and my crew. Anything you have to say can be said out loud."

Grant knew to take Big Jack seriously. When he was younger he had seen how short the man's temper was. If you could measure such a thing, his was mere centimeters. "We were just thinking about hitting the road again," Grant offered.

Big Jack pulled a chair out from the table at which they sat. His demeanor changed and his voice quieted to a threatening whisper.

"You're in my domain. I'm the fucking king here. You'll do as I say, and that includes staying or going."

Ian fought his nerves to remain in control of his body. Every inch of him wanted to shake in fear. Grant had less success in suppressing the trembles.

"Come on, Jackie, don't treat him like that. He's family!" Colleen whined from the floor. She was now lying on her side as though she hoped to nap.

Big Jack pushed the chair out and ran to her. He grabbed her arm and yanked her from the floor. "Bitch! Don't tell me how to act! You'd be dead if we hadn't opened the door for your sorry ass! And don't you fucking call me Jackie!"

"Bitch! Bitch!" Tank screamed. The altercation excited his small brain.

Colleen tore her arm away from him and ran the best she could back through the door from which she'd come out. The men could hear her sobs, but no one, not even Grant or the man that had been licking her, ran to her side.

It made Grant happy to see someone tell his mom off. She was dumb. She made poor decisions and had always lived off of the hard work of others. And she had the audacity to call him *family*. She didn't know what the word meant.

Ian was terrified and mortified that anyone would treat a woman like that. His parents had raised him better.

• • •

Was that sympathy for his mother?

"As horrible as she was, she was a person too. We all make

mistakes."

You should be as forgiving with yourself as you are with others.

"I'm working on it."

• • •

"Saddle up, everyone. Time to ride!" Big Jack roared. The men jumped to their feet, suddenly showing signs of life. A new energy rippled through the dirty bar.

"What?" Ian asked as he watched the men don their leathers and head to the front door. "You're going out there? On your bikes?"

"A bike is *never* just for show," Tank recited with a proud smile, like a child remembering to wash his hands or tying his own shoes for the first time. It must have been a rule of the club.

"What's life without the ride?" Big Jack asked. "And what's a bar without beer?"

"A beer run?" Grant asked.

"We'll stay here," Ian suggested.

"No outsiders in the club without a club member present," Tank called out. He certainly seemed to be the club's walking bylaws.

"Tank says you have to come with." Big Jack smiled maniacally. "If you want to ride with the big boys, you gotta start acting like 'em."

"We don't want to ride. We just got here and the dead are everywhere."

"If you're staying with us, what you want doesn't matter anyway."

• • •

How many red flags was it going to take for you and Grant to realize these men were bad?

"They didn't even check outside to see if it was safe."

And you still went along for the ride.

"How could we say no to Big Jack?"

• • •

The only reason the bikers survived as long as they had

was because the dead couldn't bite through all the leather. The beginning of the end for the gang started with Tank on that fateful ride. It was an unseasonably warm day and, being a heavier set man, he began to sweat quickly in the sunshine. While the other bikers looted a liquor and beer store, Tank watched the parking lot and tucked his jacket into a storage compartment on the side of his bike. A zombie approached him and Tank giggled with excitement. He raised and fist and swung to bash its face in, but his timing was off and his fist flew by in a whip of wasted energy. Tank stared at his arm, still hung in midair, in disbelief that he'd missed. A set of teeth from the spared zombie bit down into his chubby forearm.

"No no, no no no," he whimpered. He retrieved his jacket from his bike and pulled it over the wound as the boys and the others exited the store.

• • •

But you made it back to the bar and you got away.
"The bikers had a drunken meeting in a back room. We weren't allowed to attend. 'Club matters', Tank let us know. So we grabbed our bags and disappeared out the front door."
They all died in that meeting. Tank was infected. He knew it and saved you.
"Yeah, maybe they did all die. Maybe he did save us."
Speaking of getting saved, maybe we should revisit the church?
Ian sighs. Recalling the past is a trial, especially when you are judge, jury, and executioner. "The last time the dead were upon us I nearly got myself infected because…"

...I OVERESTIMATED MY STRENGTH

At this point in his young life, Ian had never played sports. He was unaware of what the inside of the school's weight room looked like and when he ran for any real distance, his asthma flared up. He had, according to Grant, the "undefined muscles of a sick girl." And hand-to-hand combat is never as easy as it looks. Nor is entering a "House of God" unprepared for what you might find within its walls. And though a church can be many things for an individual: a sanctuary, a community center, and an escape, Ian never expected the first church he entered to become a battleground.

They were moving east and still searching for food, even though their bags were full from their "friend" Thomas' generosity. Hunger threatened always to surge around the next bend, so it was best to check buildings when they could.

An auto repair shop.

"No," Grant said.

A yoga studio.

"No," he said again.

They came to a church and Ian continued walking, sure there wasn't any food to be found. When he no longer heard Grant's footsteps behind him he stopped and turned to see Grant staring at a building.

"We should check in there."

"Communion wafers have no nutritional value," Ian said and then continued walking.

"Sometimes churches have kitchens in the basement," Grant explained.

"How do *you* know anything about church?" Ian eyed him. Grant had Satanist tendencies. He was definitely closer to an earth-worshipping Pagan than he was to a Christian.

"Know thy enemy." Grant waved Ian to follow him.

The church was quiet and empty, but it was the one place they'd entered that felt okay to be empty. It looked like a weekday, instead of a Sunday, when the church would be brimming with life. They took a long hall to the back of the building and entered a room labeled *Supplies*.

Ian opened cabinet after cabinet. "Communion wafers; boxes of them. I told you."

"The body of Christ." Grant opened a box and slid a single wafer onto his tongue where it stuck and quickly absorbed all of his saliva. "Water," he said, pointing to the paste it had become.

In another cabinet, Ian found a few bottles of Dasani. "It's labeled as 'Holy'", he said. "Won't this burn your flesh?"

"Ha ha. Only one way to know." Grant held out a hand and chugged the liquid. "I'm melting!"

Ian tried a wafer and found himself downing water with his friend.

"Now, time to find the blood of Christ." Grant rubbed his hands together in expectation and his eyes were bright with excitement. That light quickly faded when he discovered that the wine cabinet was locked.

"We should leave." Ian had seen Grant drunk twice before. Both times he wanted to forget. The first ended with a near suicide attempt on a freeway overpass and the second, a girl threatening to report Grant for inappropriately touching her. Ian hoped the key was on someone's key ring, very far away.

"Come on, I really want a drink. We can hang out here; maybe sleep on pews for the night. I promise I won't cause any trouble."

"Fine," Ian said with a sigh. "The key's probably in the office."

The office—or *Secretarial Office*, as its closed door was labeled—was quiet. They knew better than to trust still air and so they each stood to one side of the door while Grant lightly tapped on the wood. Nothing. No sounds. No sudden, desperate, death-driven movements.

Ian shifted on his feet. "We've spent too much time here. Are we doing this or what?"

Grant nodded, grabbed the doorknob, and threw the door inward.

A woman rushed forward from the darkness. Her right hand was wrapped up from an old injury; the blood on the fabric had turned brown long ago. For no apparent reason, she turned toward Ian and knocked him to the ground.

An undead adversary bent on eating your flesh has even more of a want to kill you than any other thing you might come into a fight against. This statement includes sharks, grizzly bears, crocodiles, serial killers, and any fatal disease known to the CDC. A hungry zombie trumps them all. And this zombie was very, very hungry.

Ian was scared, but he wanted to prove to Grant that he could hold his own. He pushed and strained against the rotting terror. Its stomach leaked all manner of bile and rot onto his shirt. He vomited and watched in horror as the beast's biting mouth moved ever closer to his own face. He hadn't considered the ick factor, the absolute grossness of touching decay. His fingers were sinking into the woman's body, unable to push away, only able to sink in. She bent closer and her teeth dragged across the skin of Ian's neck.

"Grant! Help me!"

• • •

He was right there for you, wasn't he?
"He wrapped a banner of some kind around her face and pulled her off. Then he…he…he jumped on her head to stop her."
And he found the key and moved on like it was nothing.
"Nothing at all."

• • •

"This church is cheap," Grant observed as he inspected the label of the only wine bottle in the cabinet. "Think folks would donate more if they knew they were drinking this crap?"

They became comfortably drunk and spent the afternoon

exploring the rest of the church. The sanctuary, a room of low carpet, row after row of stiff wooden benches, and a blood stain the size of a person at the end of the center row, was empty. At the beginning of the plague, a pastor overcome by infection was re-killed by a member of his congregation. The weapon of choice had been a large cross, ripped from the wall above the altar. It now lay next to the crusted puddle of gore. A bloody trail led from the sanctuary and out the front doors.

• • •

I see you've already decided the person of whom it spilled out.
"It had to be the pastor. He'd still be here if he was alive." Ian says, unaware that not all people of God spend every waking moment at church, but also unaware that he was right.
Hardly the first blood spilled in a religious place, anyway.

• • •

The cupboards of the kitchen beneath the sanctuary were empty. On each cabinet door was posted a sign declaring "Label your food!" to any who might make use of the shelves.

As the sun went down outside, they barricaded themselves into the sanctuary.

"Pull up a pew," Grant said with a still-drunken laugh.

"Don't mind if I dewww," Ian replied, equally giddy and inebriated.

• • •

How many times has he saved your life?
"I never counted."
I bet he remembers the one time you didn't save his.
"I wasn't thinking straight."
You weren't thinking at all.
Ian jumps to his feet, anger pulsing through his frail body. He re-bundles Grant's sleeping bag, places it back near the memorial of his dead friend, and returns to his tiny closet prison.
You cannot escape me.
"I can certainly try!" Ian fumes.
This was your idea, all this story telling. Don't back out now!

"What's that noise?" Ian asks.
Don't change the subject!
"Shhh!" Ian quiets his mind. "I really do hear something."

Where earlier a cat had braved the rotting minefield of the first floor, another critter has followed. Ian hears it sniff the floor and scratch the bare wood with its small claws. His stomach growls after his mind wanders to thoughts of cooked squirrel. Grant had used early-learned hunting skills to secure a few wild meals before his death. They never really needed squirrel, but Grant liked to show off and kill things sometimes.

Ian slowly pushes the wool coat from his lap and lies down on the closet floor. He can see the bottom of a thick-furred body sitting on long feet.

A rabbit, he guesses silently.

A stench rises up in his nose and for a moment he blames the new guest on the other side of the door. But when the rabbit hops away the smell remains, digging deeper into his nostrils.

It's you.
"I gathered that, thank you," he says. He is embarrassed even though he is alone.
You smell like piss.

Catching the rabbit wouldn't help his situation much. Grant always was better with blades. Ian, on the other hand, would probably cut himself due to nervousness. He suffered paper cuts from cereal boxes and couldn't be trusted to safely open envelopes from the mail. Besides, he isn't ready to see more gore or cause the death of another living being, not yet anyway. Not *quite* starving enough. Ian does find some hope that the bunny has taken a handful of greedy fleas with it.

Sleep is calling him once more. He tries to fight it, to postpone the nightmares, but his lids are too heavy to resist.

In the middle of the cold night, Ian awakes to the tinny sound of raindrops hitting the windowpanes. For a terrifying moment his mind imagines the grotesquely long fingernails of the dead tapping on the glass. Even in their walking death as other parts rotted and fell away, their hair and nails continued to grow. Each body seems worse than the last, with curled claws extending from their fingertips.

The rain reminds you of something else.

"The day we found Thomas. It doesn't matter, he's just as alone and doomed as I am."

Everything matters, Ian. Tell them about Thomas.

"He deserved to survive, if anyone did, and he deserved our company. But…"

...I DIDN'T GIVE T.W. A CHANCE

Grant and Ian hadn't been popular in school. They weren't "in" with the sports guys or any other after school activities group. But they weren't the most unpopular either. They floated between the cliques and were generally accepted wherever they showed up. Thomas Winston existed on the outskirts of every group.

He was in a league of his own.

T.W., as he was often called, was a schoolmate of Ian's and his neighbor. He was also a young genius. A mad scientist of sorts with an interest in sketching, Thomas wore a large winter jacket year round with a breast pocket stuffed full of number two pencils and pens of every color. In the school lunchroom he drew pictures more than he ate food and most of his homework assignments were turned in with accompanying doodles in the paper margins. As memorable as he sounds, when the world ended, Ian and Grant forgot all about him until they returned to Ian's street one day to find Ian's house had been burned to the ground.

A light from an upper window of one of the houses across the street cut through the dreary, wet evening. As Ian watched it, the window opened and a figure stood backlit at the sill.

"Hey, guys! Up here!" the person called. It took the boys a second to put the voice to a name, a face.

He waved them over and pointed to a tree that grew to the right of the single-story garage. They climbed it to the first floor roof where the teen greeted them happily.

"Thomas Winston," he said with his hand in front of him, ready to shake.

"We know who you are," Grant grumbled. He had little patience for T.W.'s overly friendly personality and even less now that the world had ended. Ian, fearing immediate denial of entrance and wanting desperately to find shelter from the rain and the dead, shook Thomas' hand firmly.

"Ian, your neighbor" he introduced himself. "He's Grant."

With proper introductions made, Thomas stepped aside to let them in.

Grant climbed in first. "Holy shit!" he exclaimed. Before Ian entered, dark thoughts ran through his brain. The 'holy shit' could mean anything. Thomas could have killed his family and their bodies were rotting just inside the window. It could mean that Thomas' room was disgustingly dirty, covered in feces and moldy food. 'Holy shit' could mean that Thomas was holding a gun to Grant's head at that very moment.

"Come on, Ian," Grant coaxed. "You have to see this!"

Inside, Thomas stood to one side of his bedroom, which was clean enough for a lone teenager in the apocalypse. A bunk bed, meant for sleepovers with friends but never used as such, filled one corner and a desk sat opposite. Thomas' jacket hung on the back of the desk chair.

It was a normal room, but for the hundreds of sheets of paper covering the walls.

Every available inch of wall space had a drawing pinned or taped to it. Ian examined one closer. In it a boy with red all over him ran after a truck. A scrawled *TW* marked the bottom right corner. Another showed a large black vehicle, disabled in the middle of the street.

"He saw us take out Keller's Hummer," Grant said.

"New stuff," Thomas said. He pointed to a piece of paper that was covered in orange flames and black blobs that must have been smoke. "Retaliation." Thomas had seen Keller's destruction.

"Yeah," was all Ian could say. He was heartbroken over it, but he couldn't dwell on it.

• • •

Do you want to talk about it now? Everything you lost?
"I shouldn't. Some things aren't meant for revisiting."
You never checked the rubble. There could be something left.

"Keller probably lit that stuff on fire too."
Let's get back to T.W. for now then, but you'll have to talk about it next.

• • •

"A man of few words, many pictures." Grant was taking in as much as he could from the sketches. They told the story of what had befallen Tom and Ian's neighborhood.

"He's like a historian," Ian said.

"It's an illustrated guide to the apocalypse. Whoa, you saw aliens?" Grant asked as he pointed to a section of drawings full of green people.

Thomas shook his head and went to his desk. He dug around in a bin and pulled out the tiniest nub of a colored pencil. "I ran out of red."

"A lot of mess out there," Ian said with a sigh, thinking of the rain, the burned remains of his family's house, the bits of people all over the ground.

Thomas paced in front of his desk, deep in thought. "My parents told me to stay put until someone came for me."

"I don't know if they're coming back," Ian said as gently as he could. He knew what it was like to lose a parent and how fragile it had made him.

Thomas shrugged. "I know. But someone from the church will come for me. I'm on a list. It's part of the plan, for them to look after me. Did you see any of them coming down the road? They should be here anytime now."

Grant and Ian had seen a pair of missionaries a few blocks away, but they were no longer serving God. "No, no church people," Grant lied.

"What will you do when you run out of food?" Ian asked.

Thomas didn't answer. Instead, he led them downstairs and through a long hallway, the walls of which were covered in framed family photos. In them, Thomas sat grinning between two conservative-looking parents, both much older than Ian or Grant's.

In the kitchen, Thomas opened every cupboard door. The shelves held row after row of canned foods, from soup to vegetables to fruit medleys. Grant and Ian weren't starving in the apocalypse yet, but the food was still a sight to see. Ian's overstocked pantry, before it was burned to the ground, was slim pickings in comparison.

Ian couldn't believe his eyes. "Wow, man. You are set."

"There's more," Thomas said as he opened a door on the far end of the kitchen. It led to a garage that was just as stuffed full of food. Metal shelves held all manner of nonperishables. It was a mini mart in the middle of the neighborhood.

"Fuck." Grant shook his head as he stepped into the garage.

Ian eyed the thin, metal garage door, its face marred by several dents. There wasn't much separating them from the dead. "They don't bother you?" he asked Thomas.

"I'm quiet. They don't know I'm here. Those dents are from my dad's Buick."

"Do you think maybe we could grab a couple things?" Grant asked, but he was already reading labels and setting cans he wanted to one side of the garage.

Thomas shrugged. "Yeah, take whatever you want. Or," his voice quieted, "you could stay."

Staying with Thomas wasn't an option for either of the boys. Ian wanted to be nowhere near the remains of his home and Grant could handle no more than twenty minutes of Thomas at any given time.

"Thanks," Ian said. "Really, thanks a lot, but we need to keep moving."

Grant gave a half-assed salute. "See you around, Thomas."

Loaded down with as much food as they could carry, Grant and Ian struck out again. As they made their way down the street, Ian glanced back several times. He could see Thomas in his bedroom window, busy sketching a new piece.

"I can't imagine what would be interesting about us walking away," Ian said.

• • •

He had so much food. Someone has to say it.

"Say what?"

Don't make me say it.

"Grant's dead now, it doesn't matter. It can't be undone"

We are looking to the past. If you had stayed with T.W...

"Grant would still be alive."

Yes. And T.W. is still alive.

"We don't know that!"

You're the one who likes to write others stories how you see fit. I say he's still alive.

"No! He's dead too! Everyone is dead!" Ian bursts from the closet, but he cannot escape himself and he is forced to return when he smells the rotting bodies of Grant and Lena. He longs for the safety and security of his own home, but he cannot go back.

Because it is no more.

"And it is no more because..."

...I DIDN'T GUARD MY SANCTUARY

After countless days on the road and after Keller drove them from a house in which they were sleeping, Ian's shoes, like his patience, had worn thin. They had successfully rid their systems of the need to explore and experience the plague. The novelty had worn off and the true struggle was beginning to show through the shiny veneer they had originally seen.

Ian stared at Grant, who appeared to have aged from the stress of everything they'd been through so far. Dark bags hung beneath his eyes. "Maybe we should go home, to my house, and stay there for awhile," he suggested lightly, unsure if Grant was really feeling as tired as he looked.

"Yeah, let's," Grant replied. He turned around and headed north toward Ian's.

It wasn't out of the ordinary for them to see smoke drifting above the buildings and treetops. It was, after all, the apocalypse. Cars burned, buildings burned, *people* burned. Grant and Ian smelled like a campfire just from walking around in it.

But this cloud of smoke was different.

• • •

"It was thick, dark black."
Go on, Ian. I know it's hard.
"And it was coming from my street."
How did it make you feel?
"Warm. Too warm. Angry. Lost."

• • •

Grant and Ian could feel the heat three houses down. Flames burst from every window; no room was left untouched. As the roof collapsed, so too did Ian. He sat on the sidewalk across the street and watched his old life disappear completely. He became only a boy with a backpack and the dirty clothes that clung to his body. Interestingly, no dead were around.

He closed his eyes and remembered what it was like to walk through the front door, the way the deadbolt felt as he rotated it into the locked position. In his memory, he visited each room and tried desperately to recall every item housed within. But it was impossible to recollect each spice container his mother barely had time to use, each book his learned father had read and added to the home office library, and every action figure Ian had stored in boxes in his closet.

He began to cry.

Grant kept watch while his best friend mourned the loss of everything he called home.

• • •

He sought revenge for what you did, before burning down your house.
"Yeah, he tried to kill us first."

• • •

Keller made his move one night when they were sleeping in the dining room of another empty house. At around two in the morning, Ian awoke to a sound.

• • •

What did you hear?
"A crying baby."

• • •

The house was much colder than it was an hour earlier. Ian shook Grant, who kept his eyes closed, but turned over in his sleeping bag.

"Hmm?" he grumbled.

"Do you hear that?" Ian whispered.

"No, go back to sleep." Grant turned to face the other way once more.

The crying continued and Ian began to worry they'd missed a starving child during their earlier sweep of the house; or that others had entered while they were sleeping. Either scenario meant danger.

He crawled from his sleeping bag and walked carefully down the hall, searching the first floor for the source of the noise. In a corner bedroom, he found it.

The window was open when it hadn't been before. Frozen air flooded in. The room was empty, but propped in the windowsill was a baby monitor, turned up to full volume. He had only a moment to realize what was happening before a bright blaze in the distance caught his eyes.

• • •

I shudder to remember the sight.
"Me too."

• • •

Flaming zombies. Zombies covered in fire and walking straight for the house in which they hid, like Molotov cocktails with half a brain.

Ian dove for the monitor and ripped its batteries out, but it was too late. The dead made steady progress across the back lawn, the fire licking their decomposing flesh.

"Grant!" Ian yelled at the top of his lungs, no longer concerned about making noise. "Pack up!"

The first of the zombies hit the side of the house, transferring the fire to the dry wooden frame. A second immolated cadaver came careening through the open window. A wave of heat rushed toward Ian, inspiring him to move.

He ran into Grant, who wore his own pack and carried Ian's gear in his arms, in the hall.

"Holy shit, the house is on fire!" he said, gazing into the flame-engulfed bedroom.

Ian threw his pack on and they made their way to the fireless side of the house. They found the front door open and a crying child, the same one, called through another baby monitor set just beyond the threshold. Grant kicked it like a football and it landed on the sidewalk, shattering into several pieces. Another group of burning stiffs stumbled in their direction.

On the rooftop of the house across the street, cradling a

carefully wrapped baby doll with the other baby monitor strapped to its crying face. Keller grinned.

• • •

It was a very clever idea.
"Keller is full of them, isn't he?"

• • •

They ran for blocks, their packs bouncing on their backs, until they lost the zombie Molotovs. A gentle wind carried the scent of burnt flesh and wood.

"He's gone too far," Grant said as they stopped to catch their breath. "He could have killed us."

"I think that's the point."

• • •

"Surviving was more work than we expected."
And Keller made it harder.
"Much, much harder."
Why did he set your life on fire?
"Simply because…"

...I PISSED OFF THE WRONG GUY

Every school has a version of him: the spoiled, rich asshole who acts like he rules the world; a bully who is popular and untouchable. Of all the other kids to survive the first weeks of the apocalypse, Ian and Grant wondered most why Keller Kenton had to be one of them. He was the kind of guy who would kill his parents for the inheritance. Lucky for him, the zombies had done that dirty work and left him alone to do as he pleased.

Ian was finally beginning to feel like himself again after a major breakdown. He and Grant were starting their day at Ian's house and preparing for another foray into the surrounding neighborhood when an engine roared in the distance. Not many people were stupid enough to make such a racket. They went to a window and watched the street. A moment later a huge black hummer sped by. An untrained or desperate eye might think the vehicle belonged to the military or a special operations group, there to rescue survivors and whisk them away to a safe haven, but the boys knew otherwise.

"Looks like Keller is doing all right," Grant said, recognizing the most expensive vehicle ever to park in the student lot of the high school.

"He's going to build a crowd with that engine noise." Ian watched the end of the street where Keller's Hummer had emerged and sure enough, the dead followed.

Keller sped up the street every day for a week, bringing more and more of the undead with him each time.

• • •

He always was the leader of the pack.
"Ha. Ha. Ha," Ian droned. "It was time for payback. Keller made school hell for me."

103

You didn't take charge, though. Grant did. Again.

• • •

"We should make tomorrow his last trip," Grant said with a plan in his eyes.

"We can't kill him, Grant. He's not a zombie," Ian replied. It was an unspoken rule of theirs, that they didn't end lives unnecessarily.

"He won't die, but his tires will." Grant hefted a bucket full of nails into the kitchen from the garage. "We can break some beer bottles too and spread it out on the pavement."

Ian wasn't big on confrontation and knew a bad idea when he saw one, but it was so hard to say no to Grant and Keller really did need his ass handed to him.

• • •

The next day as Ian and Grant ate lunch, they heard the bass of Keller's music before they saw the SUV. He was right on time and the boys were ready for him. The street in front of Ian's house was covered with everything sharp they could find. Keller punched the gas and tore through the mess without second thought, making it just a few feet before the tires deflated. Keller threw the Hummer into park and jumped out.

"What the hell have you done?" Keller bellowed. He circled the Hummer, examining the shredded tires as though there might be some way to fix them. There wasn't. They were gone.

They watched from behind a large rhododendron bush in Ian's yard, listening to Keller curse as he emptied the behemoth vehicle of supplies.

"You'll pay for this, Ian!" he yelled and then took off running as the dead started to close in.

"Why am I going to pay?" Ian whined aloud. "It wasn't my idea."

"We shouldn't have destroyed his ride directly in front of your house, I suppose."

• • •

It wasn't very smart of you.

"Well, that's why it's a mistake, isn't it? Technically, it was Grant's fault."

You could have said no to the whole thing.

"That would be my mistake then, letting him go through with it."

Ian falls into a fitful sleep. His mind is filled with visions of Keller Kenton. In these terrifying dreams, Keller follows him everywhere he goes, setting ablaze the things Ian loves.

• • •

He wakes the next morning covered in sweat and burning up from the wool coat. A moment passes before Ian is sure he isn't nearly on fire once again.

You didn't only stay in houses and stores.

"I just woke up. Give me a minute."

Your time is limited.

"Ugh. No. We stayed in a hotel once too."

Because of another mistake.

"Because…"

...I CHECKED OUT

Grant and Ian traveled down a curved section of Interstate 5 to get further into Northgate's center while avoiding the zombie-infested streets of the neighborhoods. When a break in its tree-lined edges allowed, the freeway gave them a good view of the surrounding area. The permanently parked traffic offered plenty of places to hide in the form of abandoned vehicles.

It also made it extremely difficult to see all the zombies.

The Mini Cooper was the perfect height to hide the legless zombie that struggled behind it. The open door of a sedan beautifully concealed the zombie that lay across the back seat of the vehicle. There were no less than fifty biters that had ended up beneath other cars in the never-moving traffic. They lay in wait to grab ankles and chew through dirty socks. The correctional facilities van was like a jack-in-the-box or Pandora's box waiting to be opened. Four prisoners were abandoned within and now their rotting wrists were finally pulling free of the restraints.

"Watch my back," Grant said, "I'm gonna do a quick sweep through this stretch of cars. Keep your eyes on the shadows."

Ian nodded and followed behind. He was doing a good job of checking until a woman appeared out of nowhere between Grant and him. She was undead and still dressed in her work clothes. When a former nurse is decaying in her scrubs, she looks like every other nurse in the same situation. But to Ian, she could only be his mother. One foot missed a shoe and the height of the remaining one gave her an awkward up-and-down lurch as she gained on Grant. The bobbing of her body was mesmerizing to Ian, setting him into a trancelike state as she drew closer to his friend.

She reached her arms out and grabbed hold of Grant's hair in one hand and his left arm in the other. In Ian's mind he could see his mother's urine-stained pants, her stringy hair, and the hunger in her eyes. He wanted her to be happy, fed.

"Ian!" Grant yelled as he struggled to get away from the zombie.

Ian stood still and let the tears fall from his eyes. If his friend had to die for his mother to be satisfied, he couldn't find the strength to disallow it.

• • •

Your track record is ridiculous.

"Grant could have died then. I was going to let him."

It might have been better. Less your fault than Lena. A death you could live with.

"No, I still didn't help when I should have. It was absolutely my fault."

But you wouldn't be stuck in the closet if he had died sooner.

• • •

"Ian, what the fuck?" Grant screamed. He managed to push the woman off and trap her in a car. Her fingernails pulled from their beds and stuck to the rear window as she clawed at the glass. Grant shook uncontrollably from the close call.

"I'm sorry," Ian said distantly. "Things are catching up with me."

Drawn by Grant's voice, zombies came from every direction in the pileup, tumbling between the cars like pinballs in a machine. He grabbed one of Ian's shoulders and led him to a Vanagon with tinted windows. After a quick scan for any undead inside, they climbed in and closed the door. A few revenants bumped up against the sides of the vehicle, but they soon lost interest when no flesh was to be found.

"Hey, I know you lost your mom and that makes you sad, but there isn't room for these emotions in the apocalypse." Grant checked his clothes for tears and any pieces of the zombie that might have transferred during their scuffle. He found a slimy fingernail on his shoulder and flicked it away with a grimace.

Ian didn't respond. He was in shock and his mind still

replayed the last images he had of his undead mother. A soccer ball slowly lost air on the floor of the vehicle. Grant picked it up and threw it at Ian's chest to break him from his daze.

"What?" Ian asked, unsure of where they were and what they were doing there.

Grant leaned back against the side of the Vanagon and closed his eyes. "We need to find somewhere secure to stay for awhile. I can't depend on you right now."

• • •

You know, Grant is really looking like the better friend here.
"He already knew loss. His mother was a waste of life, his dad was a deadbeat. He had a pet snake when he was nine, but it was sick when he got it and it died."
Did you just say that Grant is a better friend because his snake died?
"Don't be a dick. You know what I mean! Bad things never happened in my life before this."

• • •

Instead of traveling east toward the central part of the city suburb, Grant and Ian took the long ramp of Exit 173 and turned west behind a gas station. They cut through a car wash tunnel. The scrubbers hung sadly, waiting to have purpose again.

"Where are we going?" Ian asked. "This is kind of the long way back to my house."

"Do you honestly think you need to be anywhere near your house right now? It's full of memories of your mom and dad. We're going to the hotel." Grant trudged up a steep embankment into the parking lot of the Hotel Nexus.

The hotel was an old four-story, 169-room behemoth of a building on Northgate Way, recently given a modern makeover through paint and furnishing changes. It was full of dangerous possibilities, but Grant was willing to risk it for the easily secured and comfortable shelter a room on the fourth floor would provide. Once when he was younger, Ian stayed at the hotel with his parents when their house was bug-bombed. He remembered it as clean and with a friendly staff. Now, he found himself hoping it had become a spotless ghost town.

Grant made for the lobby doors, but he stopped and held a hand to Ian's chest. "You should take the stairs to the fourth floor and wait for me."

Ian was scared to go alone, but he was frightened of the lobby as well. He beheld the tower that led to the long hallways of the upper floors. A handful of the doors were open, some all the way, some only a crack.

"Lots of places for things to hide."

"I'll be right behind you," Grant said. "We have to get a master key. The electronic locks won't work."

Ian jogged to the stairwell. The dead were moving toward them from across the street. He hit each step as quietly as possible and took frequent breaks for his breath and Grant to catch up. They stood at the top floor railing and viewed the parking lot from above.

"A lot of cars down there." Grant took a deep breath. "There could be folks hiding out in the rooms still. Late check outs." He smiled.

"Yeah, we'll have to pick carefully."

• • •

You found a room no problem.

"I can still remember the smell of the shampoo."

That place was nice. You should have stayed there. Grant was still alive then.

"Can't I finish my story without you bringing that up?"

• • •

"Wow." Grant threw his bag on the ground and walked deeper into the room. There was a kitchen stocked with cooking utensils, a dining area, a flat screen television and a comfortable couch. He fell onto one of the double beds, its bedding still tucked perfectly beneath the mattress. Ian followed suit, taking the second bed.

• • •

"Those beds were amazing."

They were plain, old beds. They're just better than a wood floor of a closet.

110

• • •

"It's like an apartment."

From the other bed Grant sighed. "I could stay here for a while."

Ian stood up. "Help me put the couch in front of the door."

"The zombies won't get up here."

"The others, in the other rooms. They could take our stuff in the night."

That evening, from the window of the hotel room, Ian watched crooked shapes wander in the moonlight. Each form a demented, interpretive dancer with unfailing energy.

"We can go outside, Ian, on the deck," Grant suggested. "They aren't gonna take the elevator."

"There's a lot of them in the street. I don't want to end up trapped. Even if they can't make it up here, we still have to make it down."

"Whatever you say, man."

• • •

Remember the maid?
"She was scarier than the zombies."

• • •

On the second day of their stay in the suite, around midday, the sound of wheels rolling down the outdoor hallway broke the silence. Grant peeked out the large window and saw a hotel maid rolling her cart toward their room. He moved the couch, opened the door before she could try, and stepped out. Ian listened from his bed.

"We don't want to be disturbed."

"I brought you some fresh towels," the maid responded.

"That is *very* disturbing. Why are you here, working?"

She handed him a small stack of clean towels. "My boss didn't tell me not to come so I'm watching after the hotel."

"But if no one's here, what are you doing?"

"I've been making my way through the building, checking all

the rooms. Some of them are in very bad shape. I'm almost done. I'm about to clean the one next door."

They watched the woman go about her work. First, she dragged a man's body from the room and placed it on a low cart. Ian wondered why she didn't throw the body over the railing, but then realized it would splatter all over the parking lot, and the maid's duty was to clean, not to make a mess.

"This one shot himself." She shook her head. "Big mess to clean up. Time for the tough chemicals."

Next she brought out the dirty linens. First the man's used towels, wrinkled and slightly wet, but not bloody. Then she pulled on latex gloves, disappeared back into the room and came out carrying pillowcases and a bed sheet, all covered in blood and bits. She put them in the same bag with the other laundry.

"Oh, don't worry," the maid exclaimed when she saw the looks of disgust on Ian and Grant's faces, "you'd be surprised what we've gotten out of the sheets."

• • •

"She cleaned the entire room as though it'd see guests again."

It's good to have a purpose in life. Maybe that's something you can find for yourself?

"I'm not gonna clean hotel rooms."

A purpose, not that purpose.

Ian shakes his head as though he can rid it of the voice inside.

• • •

"Do you boys need anything else? The ice machine and hot tub don't work, but there's a game room with a pool table and some snacks in the employee lounge. It's safe down there."

"No, we're good. Thanks," Grant replied.

She glanced at her watch, which Ian saw as an archaic behavior. "When will you be checking out?"

"He already has." Grant pointed a thumb at Ian, who smacked it away.

Ian shrugged. "We never checked in."

The maid smiled and rolled her carts, linen and limb laden,

one in front of her and one behind, down the hall and out of sight.

• • •

They stayed in the hotel room for a week while Ian battled nightmares and anxiety. During the daytime, Grant searched the nearby buildings, an Indian restaurant, a Starbucks, two gas stations, and a 7-11 for anything they might be able to use. He also found the room where the maid was storing the collected bodies. Not all of them were dead again.

Over dinner in the hotel room one night, Ian threw in the towel. "Grant, I'm done with this."

Grant reached across the table to take the leftovers from his friend.

"Not my food! I'm done with adventuring. I need to stay home, or here."

"No! Fuck that! Life was dangerous and hard even before zombies existed. People died all the time from car accidents, plane crashes, and all sorts of shit. If anything, life has gotten easier. I'm leaving and I'm not leaving without you!"

• • •

"So we went."

It was always hard for you to say no to him.

"The apocalypse stayed fun for him a lot longer than it did for me."

You had another kind of moment before that.

"I got very, very sick, because…"

Michelle Kilmer

...I DIDN'T EAT MY FRUITS AND VEGGIES

Proper nutrition isn't a concern for most young adults. Serving sizes, food pyramids and sugar intake are taught and mentioned by the school and a caring mother or two, but they are ignored whenever possible. Dwindling choices also hamper the task of eating right. Therefore, before the boys made it into the city center and closer to better food supplies, they subsisted on ramen noodle cups, bags of chips and soda; a typical teenage boy diet.

• • •

Tell them what it did to you.

• • •

After another day of exploring in the surrounding neighborhood, Ian and Grant were unpacking their loot in the living room of Ian's house. A freshly made zombie, searching for sustenance, stumbled down the side yard and happened to see the boys moving around inside. It careened into the window with the ignorance of a bird, desperate to consume them, but not realizing glass blocked its path.

"Shit!" Grant yelled. "Grab your bag, let's get upstairs!" He ran to the stairwell with his own gear and flew up the stairs, leaving Ian alone.

Light-headedness hit Ian like a punch to the stomach, sudden and debilitating. His hand refused to close around the strap of his backpack. He tried again and again, but finally chose to abandon his gear when a second zombie joined the first at the window. His legs felt heavy and he pulled against gravity with all of his might to reach the foot of the stairs. Thinking that crawling might be easier, he dropped to his hands and knees. The new position allowed him to ascend the first flight of stairs, but when he reached the landing before the second set, his vision blurred and he fell into

Michelle Kilmer

unconsciousness.

When he awoke, a quilt kept him warm on his bed. The sun rose on the distant horizon and Ian could make out Grant's form in the chair at his desk. He slept with his head on the hardwood tabletop.

• • •

Did you expect to see him there?

"Honestly, no. But I think that was out of confusion. If the world had been normal, he'd have gone home. When I woke up, it took me a moment to remember how fucked up everything was."

• • •

"Grant," Ian managed to croak. Dryness clung heavy to his throat as though it sought to choke him from the inside. His head ached.

Across the room, Grant stirred, but didn't wake.

"Hey!" Ian yelled as loud as he could. His friend woke, rubbed crusty bits of sleep from his eyes, and came to sit on the edge of the bed.

"You look like shit," Ian said to him.

"Well, I fucking feel like it too. Last night was rough." Grant lay down, opposite of Ian, with his head at the foot of the bed. "You also look like shit, by the way."

Ian's sick body and tired mind couldn't remember anything about the night before. "What happened?"

"You passed out on the stairs. I had to drag you up here."

Ian felt his temperature rising; a fever was taking hold of him. He remembered they were unpacking. He remembered, "the zombies!"

"It's okay," Grant said as he propped himself up on one arm. "They're gone now. I was trying to figure out what to do with them when a raccoon crossed the backyard. They broke through a section of the fence to follow it."

Ian relaxed. "Lucky."

"Yeah." Grant lay back down, his neck stiff from sleeping at the desk.

"Why do you think I blacked out?"

"I'm guessing it has something to do with the fact that we've been eating air, sugar and salt for weeks. When was the last time you had water?"

"I had a soda yesterday. There's water in that, right?"

"The bad stuff in it outweighs the good. We aren't doing this right. It's catching up to us. "

"Lay off, Grant." Ian struggled to sit up against the headboard. "I'm not the only one ignoring the cans of vegetables."

"It's not just vegetables. We need more variety. And I'm feeling run down too."

"Are you saying that three kinds of Doritos doesn't count as variety?" Ian laughed and Grant laughed with him.

That night, Ian's fever raged. His legs ached and his skin burned fiery hot.

• • •

"I miss that warmth."

It was nice, wasn't it?

"Much nicer than this," Ian says through chattering teeth. Another night has come in the closet. The cold air bites at him like the teeth of the dead might if they find him.

You can take a break, go to sleep.

"No, the story isn't over yet."

• • •

Nightmares of the apocalypse are frightening, but fever dreams of the apocalypse are far worse. In the height of his febrility, Ian saw his mother. Even though she was still undead, she bustled about his bedroom as she had in life, tending to her sick son. When she was alive she would stay at his side until he was diagnosed, treated, and cured of whatever ailed him. To her, a bug bite that wouldn't stop itching was as serious as pneumonia. Ian's sick mind envisioned her equally devoted in her undeath. She brought him chicken noodle soup, but pus dripped into the bowl from wounds on her face. She felt his forehead, but the cold flesh of her dead

Michelle Kilmer

hand shocked him and he tore away from it. The cough syrup she forced him to gulp looked and tasted suspiciously like blood. It was when she came into his room with a rag and bucket to wash him, its thin metal handle cutting into her wrist and its warm water causing the skin to slough off of her hands, that he finally broke free from the nightmare.

Ian cried out from beneath his sweat-soaked sheets. He frantically searched the room for a sign of his mother, anxious to keep her from cleaning him and determined to avoid drinking any more of the bloody cough syrup. He began to sob out of fear and sadness. Part of him wanted to see his mother, alive or undead.

"Mom?" The tears fell freely down his face, joining the beads of sweat there.

Grant, who was asleep in Ian's parents' bedroom down the hall, heard his crying and came back to his friend's side. "She's gone, Ian."

"So, she was here?" Again, but this time hopefully, he sought any recent sign of his mother. There on the nightstand, an uneaten bowl of soup sat cold. A wrung out rag hung sadly over the back of a chair to dry. But there was no proof. Instead he saw a note she'd written in fifth grade wishing him good luck on a presentation, a picture they'd taken together at the science center downtown when he was thirteen, and last year, her hands made the very quilt he lay under. These memories were much too old. She hadn't been in his room in a long time.

"You were imagining things. You're still really sick."

"I didn't get to say goodbye. She was here and then she was just…gone."

"You did the next best thing to saying goodbye. You tried to find her and you did. Now, take two of these and stop crying like a baby." He threw a plastic bottle of Tylenol at Ian.

"I want my mom, Goddammit!" He turned away from Grant dramatically, sending the Tylenol bottle rolling off onto the floor.

Grant couldn't understand what it was like to miss a mother. He picked up the bottle, removed two white pills, and shoved them

118

in Ian's face. "Take them or I'll put you outside with the wolves. I'm sick of your whining and you need to get better. We have places to go and zombies to see."

"I don't want to see more zombies," Ian said.

"Just take the freaking pills already!" Grant left the room, unwilling to argue with Ian any further.

Ian grudgingly did as he asked and to his surprise, the little pills helped immensely. By that night he could sit up and keep down soup. The nightmares of his undead mother took a while longer to leave him.

"So, what kind of food do we need to find?"

"No more snack food. We need breakfast, lunch and dinner. We need meat and vegetables."

A word about meat in the apocalypse: no one was eating it fresh besides the zombies. There were no more Big Macs, no more steak dinners or barbecue. Other than canned Vienna sausages, beef jerky, dehydrated meals, smoked salmon, and tinned sardines (if you were lucky enough to find any of this stuff), the only opportunity to consume was wild animals and they were near impossible to catch.

• • •

Didn't Grant have a beef jerky bag in his pack?
"It's empty. Grant ate it all a long time ago."
Did you check the bottom of the bag? There are always those little pieces left over.
Ian crawls out of the closet in the dark and makes his way back to the pile of Grant's things. He finds the jerky bag and dumps the tiny, but flavorful nuggets into his mouth. Back in the closet he cares not that the dehydrated meat is stuck between his teeth.

He falls asleep happily enough with the taste of beef in his mouth and dreams of savoring a burger, and though it pains him when he wakes up...

"I'm thankful I didn't dream of my mother."
Especially since it's time to talk about her a lot more.

"It was a horrible mistake. I should have done it sooner. But it was too late when…"

...I TRIED TO SAY GOODBYE

Grant's mother was mostly absent, drugged out when she was present, and generally a lousy mom, whereas Ian's mother was caring, attentive, and always had time for Ian if he needed it. Because of this healthy relationship with his mother, Ian wanted her to know that he was still alive. Because of the love he felt for her, he needed to know that she was alive. So, against everything he knew to be safe and against Grant's wishes, he went to the hospital to find her.

They entered the cemetery first, located across the street, in eerily convenient proximity to the hospital. Being mostly empty of the undead, it was a welcome respite. There, in the silent space of a mausoleum, Ian planned his foray into the medical building.

"I'm not sure you'll make it inside," Grant said as he lazily traced the engraved lines of a plaque on the wall with his dirty fingers. "It's one of the worst places to go."

Ignoring Grant's lack of faith, Ian dug through his memories of the entrances, hallways, reception areas, and rooms he'd seen so many times before. "She works on the second floor."

He drew a map on a scrap of paper of what he thought was the best route. The emergency room entrance wasn't an option. It was ground zero for the apocalypse. He also nixed the idea of using the main entrance as he imagined needing to pry the doors open. A first floor window around the back of the hospital would have to do.

"That's a lot of running," Grant commented, surveying Ian's poorly drawn path.

"Grant, I need to do this! Please stop saying negative stuff." Ian folded the map, but didn't pack it away. He would need to refer to it as he kept the dead off of his heels. "You're giving me doubts."

• • •

Ian reaches around in the dim closet for his backpack. He still has the map, folded in a side pocket and though he cannot see the lines, he finds comfort in touching the paper.

You kept it.

"I don't have anything else to remind me of my mom."

Do you really want to remember her like that? She was disgusting.

"Stop it! She couldn't help it! And you're fucking giving shit away again!"

Fine, back to the story.

• • •

The boys set out across the rest of the cemetery, cutting through the grass and over shallow grave markers. Several of Ian's relatives were buried there, but it never crossed his mind to pay his respects. He only imagined their skeletons, struggling in their coffins, somehow brought back to this world like the rest of the dead. At the north end of the block, they could see one of the hospital's parking lots, the parking attendant's shack, and the winding driveway that led beyond both and into the complex itself.

Bodies, moving and non-moving, dotted the landscape. The dead were everywhere.

"Hah! Zombie butt!" Grant laughed as he pointed to an undead man in nothing but a loosely tied hospital gown.

Ian smiled. It was a funny sight.

They approached the parking attendant's shack. No blood, no weapons either. On one side of the seat was a bag of unopened beef jerky.

Grant nearly drooled. "I'll be in here," he said.

"You aren't coming?" Ian asked. "The hospital is big. I'll need your help."

"I can't, Ian. I hate hospitals," Grant said as he slid open the shack's door. It wasn't a lie. He'd spent time in the ER with his father and mother, dealing with trauma from a motorcycle accident and an overdose, respectively.

"Fine." Ian took a deep breath and exhaled as he sprinted toward the back of the hospital. Only two zombies hung around at the far end of the rear parking lot. *Get inside*, he reminded himself. He hugged the building and walked through the untrimmed grass beneath the first floor windows.

Thunk. A dead woman threw herself against the glass of her hospital room. She bit at the window, leaving saliva and several teeth there. Thin plastic tubes still ran from her arm to bags that hung on a pole behind her. As Ian continued down the building, she followed him along the wall until she reached the corner of her room. The window of the room next door was cracked open. He pressed his face to the pane and looked inside, half fearing another biter would spring up and gnaw at the idea of his flesh. From what he could see, the room was empty. He opened it halfway and climbed into the room. There wasn't much he could use as a weapon, but Ian did find an unopened bottle of water that he threw in his pack. He glanced into the hallway and was surprised to see it empty. The hospital was full of the dead; they were just somewhere else at that moment.

The hall led him through several wards. Ian was becoming used to the gore and grossness of the infected, but there he saw the evil of the living and it was unbearable to witness. In an area for terminal patients, ampoules of potassium chloride had been emptied into syringes and those syringes emptied into them as they were going to die anyway. In the difficult existence of the apocalypse, the slowly dying were burdens, baggage that couldn't be carried or walked out. *Did my mother have a hand in this?* He wondered. It was an impossible thought, but she was known among the staff as someone who made "the hard decisions".

In the Infant Ward, bloody prints covered the window that allowed observation of the newborn room. Inside, Ian could see what the dead had been seeking. Several infants, dead from starvation and reanimated, squirmed in the incubators. Desperate cries, cries that a bottle wouldn't end, crawled from their small chests. Their rotting stomachs were hungry for something else.

• • •

"They'd barely known life. They'd spent more time undead, than alive."

Now that's something to be thankful for, in your case. Isn't it?

"No, not at all. I'd swap spots in a second to not know this suffering."

And there were others in the room?

• • •

A family, the mother still clutching her tiny child, sat dead in a corner. The male, whom Ian could only assume was the father, loosely held a handgun. A bullet to the brain for the whole clan, recently two made three. Ian was happy then that Grant hadn't come. He would want to grab the gun, but the door was blocked from the inside and they couldn't risk the noise of breaking in. It wasn't the reason Ian was there anyway and a room full of zombie infants, wiggling and chomping their toothless mouths, was a nightmare he didn't want to hold onto.

He continued down the long corridor, using empty laundry bins and food carts stacked with trays of rotting food as cover. In the stairwell, he sat for a moment. There would be more corpses on the second floor, especially with the Intensive Care Unit taking up most of that level. His mother would not have left her post as an ICU nurse. She had to be up there. His cell phone, which he stubbornly still carried, didn't work, so he couldn't call or text her. Even if it did work, he couldn't risk ringing her up and attracting zombies to her location. The generator still pumped power to the second floor of the building, which meant that the intercom might work, if he managed to locate it. The risk with this of course was inviting the dead to come to him. Still, it was safer than searching the entire second floor, room by room.

At the stairwell door to the second floor, Ian peered through the square window at another empty hall in front of him. It was unsettling, but he felt thankful for his luck. He pulled open the door and walked straight to the nurses' station without trouble of any kind.

He took the phone in his hand, examined it and his thoughts, unsure of whether he was ready for the answer he might receive, and pressed the button labeled Intercom.

"Mom?" His voice boomed in the emptiness. He felt stupid for using precious airtime on three letters that could mean so much to many. Should he say her name so she knew he meant her? Or his?

"This is Ian." Again, he felt idiotic.

Footfalls and moans echoed from around a corner. They were coming. He recradled the phone, crouched low behind the desk, and waited. Fortunately, or unfortunately, Ian had a good view of a circular security mirror that hung near the nurses' station. It afforded him a reflection of the approaching chaos.

• • •

"I don't want to tell this part."
You don't have that choice. It could be the key to getting better. You can't leave out a word.
"She was right there, right in front."

• • •

He saw her.

She had found him, but the reunion was not as he imagined. Drawn by his voice, but not *his* voice, only a sound above other sounds, she walked with two other corpses, a patient and a janitor, at the front of the pack. His mother's hair was stringy and caked with blood. She shuffled like a woman forty years her senior. Urine and feces stained her white pants.

"Mom," Ian called as he began to cry.

• • •

No one should have to see a parent like that.
"Ha," Ian scoffs, "ya think?"
How did it make you feel?
"Like a part of me had died."
Like it later felt to lose Grant?
"No, a million times worse. Like I didn't have a right to exist anymore."

• • •

The undead continued to gather, their moaning attracting more from other areas of the hospital. He watched the crowd thicken until it was ten rotting bodies deep and twenty across. One of them would soon find the swinging quarter door that led behind the desk. They would all follow, like water rushing in through opened floodgates, and eat him alive.

Another nurse, maybe one who had worked behind the station, was breaking free of the group and making her way to the door. Ian closed his eyes and hugged his knees, preparing for the pain. He heard the hinges squeak.

Then, an explosion rocked the building. Windows shattered in the rooms across the hall. The dead began to move away from Ian and toward any exit that would bring them closer to the noise. The nurse who was on the verge of discovering him followed the others like a bird in migration. Ian let a few minutes pass before moving even a finger. When he thought they were gone, he slid across the linoleum on his belly until he reached the quarter door. A maggot squirmed on its top edge, left there by the dead hospital employee. He watched it wiggle for a brief moment; a symbol of how close he'd come to death.

He took the stairs back down to the first floor and sprinted for the back lot. Grant was waiting for him there, grinning like a maniac.

"Dude, I blew up a car!" Grant yelled.

"You saved my life."

• • •

He saved your life.

"Don't rub it in."

You didn't save his.

"I told you to drop it."

And he thought nothing of saving it. What did he say again?

"You should have seen the fireball," Ian says in a voice devoid of emotion.

He said it much more enthusiastically.

126

• • •

"You should have seen the fireball!" Grant exclaimed. "It was huge!"

Traveling back to Ian's house that afternoon was slow going. He dragged his feet and turned back several times to look at the hospital. The boys usually traveled quietly, but Grant was so pumped from the explosion that he retold the rescue story over and over.

"I could hear the intercom out here and the zombies could too. They came from every direction! It was like you rang a dinner bell! I saw the minivan and I knew I had to do something to get them moving away from you. You know that lighter I always carry around? Well, I ripped the shirt off a dead guy and stuffed it in the gas tank. It lit up so quick I had to bolt outta there! I've never run that fast!"

Ian had no energy to respond so he allowed Grant to talk until he grew angry that Ian wasn't participating in the conversation.

Back at home, Ian stood in his parents' walk-in closet. He stared at his mother's stockpile of multi-colored scrubs. He remembered the urine stains down her legs. She was scared when she died.

And that scared him.

• • •

"She isn't dead. She just can't be!"
Denial is a stage of grief. It might be time to move to another stage.
"I don't know any of the other stages." Ian tries to remember something he read in one of his father's books. "But I remember something nice about my mom."
Tell them about it then.

• • •

His previous last memory of her was Friday night's dinner, the evening before the plague came to town. His father was working late at his office so his mother cooked Ian's favorite dinner of macaroni and cheese and let him rent a movie online. It was a near perfect evening, as though the universe was giving him the best before replacing it with the worst. It was also one of the rare occasions in which Ian saw his mother in regular clothes. She wore jeans and a blouse instead of her scrubs. To him, she looked how a mom should look: happy and normal.

• • •

That is nice.

"And then I had to go and fucking screw it up! I insisted on saying goodbye and now my final memory of her is forever altered. She is dirty, disgusting and dead!"

You need to try to forget.

"It will haunt me for the rest of my life. I pray that isn't long."

"Ian! Grant!" a familiar voice calls from the front lawn.

"It's Keller," Ian tells himself. "What do I do?"

Stay quiet. He'll think Lena killed you both.

"So you believe me now, that he sent her?"

I have accepted it as part of your reality.

"I should face him. I know where all the weapons are now."

You are in no shape to fight him. He'll kill you.

"I'm dying anyway," Ian says as he stands up in the closet. The wool coat falls to the floor. An empty water bottle and the bodies of moth larvae crunch and squish under his feet.

Listen to me! Don't you dare let him know you are here. You've ignored me before.

"Ignoring you is the one thing I'm good at."

Why don't you sit back down and tell them about that then?

...I DIDN'T TRUST MY GUT

In fact, Ian did a pretty good job of ignoring it entirely. The little voice inside his head said *stay home, stay in the place that you know, stay safe*. But he and Grant were itching to get out and explore. He wanted to see the inside of some of the other houses in his neighborhood and now the opportunity was before him. Besides, if you could get away with looting, wouldn't you?

Their plan was to make ever-larger circles, block-by-block, but to always end up back at Ian's house. Sometimes they would make it back before dark. Other times they might have to find a place to sleep and head back the next day.

"Where should we go first?" Grant asked as he rubbed his hands together mischievously.

Ian scrutinized the front door, which his mind told him danger was on the other side, but all he wanted to do was open it. "My neighbor Gerry's on a hunting trip. He probably won't make it home. We could check his house for supplies." He didn't expect Grant to say yes.

"Okay!" Grant said, jumping up from the couch. "Grab your gear!"

Grant had several trespassing citations under his belt. He was no stranger to angry owners and responding cops. Once, he'd climbed the fence that blocked the delivery area underneath the mall and another time he was caught shooting his BB gun into the trees on cemetery property. But Ian wasn't a rule-breaker and he had qualms about breaking and entering.

They hopped the fence between the two backyards. Grant wrapped his hand in a t-shirt and punched a hole through a window in the back door. He unlocked the deadbolt and walked in.

"Easy," he said. "Now, let's find some goodies."

• • •

And I told you to turn back, didn't I?
"But I didn't. I followed him in."

• • •

Camping gear lay scattered about the living room, as though someone had just come home from a trip rather than left for one.

"Does he always leave his gear out like this? It's like he wants someone to take it."

It would have been easier for Ian to touch things that weren't his if they didn't belong to someone he knew. He instead looked at the photos on a wood-paneled wall across from the couch. Gerry had several grown children and, from the many faces in the images, a plethora of grandchildren.

"This machete is nice. You should take it." Grant picked up the black-bladed weapon and swung it through the air, attacking an invisible creature there.

Ian stepped back. When Grant was excited, sometimes he wasn't careful. He'd once hit Ian in the face with an Xbox controller when he died in a game. "Maybe this isn't a good idea."

Grant held the blade out to him. "Take it. Once you know how good it feels, you won't want to put it down."

• • •

I told you not to.
"But I held it and it felt great, just like Grant said."

• • •

"Who's there?" a man called from down the hall. His voice was coarse as though he'd just woken up or recently spent too much time screaming. He emerged from a back room. "What the hell are you doing in my house?"

It was Gerry, but he seemed different to Ian. The man's skin was ghost white and his left arm was generously wrapped in multiple gauze bandages.

"Um, uh…my mom wanted me to check on you." Ian hoped the old man would buy the lie.

"I'm…not okay." He held up his arm. "Had to come home

130

early, say my goodbyes."

As far as Ian knew, Gerry lived alone and his family was spread out across the country. "We'll be going then."

The sick man stumbled as he walked toward the wall of photos. Ian still held the machete. Grant stared at Gerry. Ian knew it was because Grant wanted to see the change occur. But they both noticed the gun tucked into his belt.

Gerry brought two fingers to his lips and kissed them. He then placed the fingers on a face in one of the images. He repeated the gesture over and over, until every loved one was accounted for. With the same hand he then reached for his gun.

• • •

I told you to run.
"But I didn't. I watched a man take his own life."

• • •

The sound of the gunshot and the instantaneous spray of blood and brain matter onto the white popcorn ceiling made the boys jump. Ian dropped the machete. Grant still stared at Gerry in amazement.

• • •

You could have avoided the entire situation, all of this, if you'd only listened to me.
"I could have avoided seeing all the dead little kids at the elementary school, their abandoned backpacks and tiny shoes, the way the returned ones wandered around like drunken sailors. That one girl whose hands were worn to stumps from clawing at the classroom door. The teacher who hanged herself on the basketball hoop. And Grant, and Ripley, and my parents! It's all so fucked up!" Ian stands and punches the closet walls around him. One of the strikes opens a hole to the room next door. He clutches his hair in clumps and sinks back down to the floor. *Breathe, Ian. Calm down. You're rocking like a crazy person. Tell them why you ignored me.*
"I didn't trust my gut because…"

...I THOUGHT I WAS SAFE

Due to his parents' professions, the house he grew up in, before it burned, was fully stocked with first aid kits and self-help books. Because they both worked long hours, the pantry was brimming with non-perishables for Ian to prepare for himself. When the world started to end, Ian assumed his parents would continue to look out for him. He still felt he could come home to a clean bed, his choice of snacks, and sack lunches.

On a Saturday, Ian woke to an empty house. His Mom was already gone at the hospital and his Dad was at his office. They were creatures of habit and bound by their respective duties. He went downstairs to the kitchen, still in his pajamas, and poured himself a bowl of cereal. One of his parents had left the television on, but the sounds it was emitting were indiscernible over the loud crunching of his Cocoa Puffs. He put his dirty bowl by the sink and sat down for his usual morning cartoon run. Technically, he was too old for the programming, but he wasn't quite ready to grow up yet.

As soon as he sat down his ears zeroed in on the word 'plague' coming from an anchorwoman's mouth. The ticker across the bottom of the screen threw out words like 'attack', 'unknown origin', 'terrorism', and 'contagious'. When Ian reached for the remote, desperate to hear as much as he could, he found a note from his mother taped to its surface.

Please put the laundry in the dryer and keep the doors locked. - Love Mom

• • •

Even your Mom couldn't save you. She tried though, didn't she?
"She always did."
She was a good mom.

133

"To more than me. That's why she went to the hospital that day and never came back."

• • •

Ian knew his parents would both be overwhelmed and maybe not make it home to him that first night. His mother would be treating people wounded out of fear. His father would get all sorts of crazy people in his office, saying crazier things than they previously had. He felt no need to switch the laundry at that moment. He'd get to it before they came back.

He ran up the stairs to his room and changed out of his sleepwear. His cell phone chirped and he picked it up to find it had filled with texts from Grant. The gist of the messages was that he was on his way over and 'dressed to kill', which Ian correctly interpreted as apocalyptic humor. Ian was on his way to the pantry when Grant let himself in, which was not out of the ordinary, especially on a weekend. He had donned a t-shirt that read *Zombies just want hugs*. Ian had selected his *Dawn of the Dead* shirt and they smiled when they noticed the similar choices. Grant had a huge duffel bag that was nearly as long as he was tall.

"What's in the bag?" Ian asked.

"Everything," Grant replied and he meant it. His possessions were few, even before the end of the world. "But I could use something to eat."

Ian pointed to the kitchen. "You saw the news then?"

Grant nodded, poured himself his own bowl of cereal and they walked to the living room. They scanned the channels and watched the programming drop like flies. One station after the next turned to static or the Emergency Broadcast Signal.

• • •

And yet you still felt safe.

"Suburbia and privilege have a way of doing that to you. It felt fun to pretend it was real."

The world around you was already a mess though.

• • •

The Seattle Center was a blood bath and the fountain at its

center ran red. Riots raged downtown. Folks hauled away clothing and electronics from shops with broken windows, only to be devoured a block down and their treasure taken by another before they too were attacked. The video switched to a busload of tourists on a Ride the Duck amphibious vehicle. They were stuck in traffic and surrounded by the dead, but luckily just out of arms reach as the vehicle was elevated. Terror clung to their faces.

"Its like a bento box on wheels," Grant said. "They'll be nice and juicy when the infected finally reach 'em."

"Gross."

When all but one station remained, Ian stood up and stretched. "Let's move upstairs, we can ride this out there."

They hauled as much as they could to the hallway at the top of the stairs and then into his parents' bedroom. Back down in the garage, they searched for weapons. The sledgehammer was too heavy to swing with enough stopping force, so they chose a hammer from Ian's dad's unused toolbox and a wooden baseball bat.

"We should bring up the camping gear. At least the lanterns and camp stove in case the power goes out." Grant held up a sleeping bag.

"Good idea." They found several flashlights as well and Ian dug through the pantry for extra batteries.

"Wow, this is a great view." Grant stood in front of a large window overlooking the front yard and street. "We can see everything."

Ian hated spending time in his parents' bedroom and didn't like thinking about them as a loving couple. It had been a long time since he'd seen any proof of that relationship, but Grant was right, the view was unbeatable. From there they could keep tabs on the goings on in his neighborhood. It was the perfect tower base camp.

They watched other families attempt to leave their homes or secure them against invasion. Ian recognized some of the kids. He was sure his parents knew the adults.

Ian and Grant laughed at the fear on their faces.

• • •

"It was wrong of us, insensitive."
You know that fear now.
"Too well."

• • •

"They won't last a week," Grant said. "We will though. We're gonna live like kings while we do too."

Across the street, a "Happy Birthday" balloon bobbed above a mailbox. Then the front door of the house behind it opened.

"Look," Ian said, pointing to the door. A woman ran from the house, blood poured from her neck and she tried in vain to stop the flow. A small, pale boy followed behind her. His face was covered in blood. He caught up to her at the sidewalk and bit her again, this time on her leg. He chewed on her flesh for a moment, but lost interest when she stopped moving.

Grant's knees wobbled.

The hair on the back of Ian's neck was raised.

Both boys felt their hearts begin to pump faster from excitement.

"Is that what I think it is?" Ian asked.

"Fuck!" Grant yelled. "It's fucking here!"

Seeing the carnage on television was nothing in comparison to those front row seats.

Ian sat down at the foot of his parents' bed. "Oh my God."

"That, right there, is a zombie, Ian!"

• • •

From then on, they watched the number of corpses in the street multiply.

• • •

It was a sight to behold.
"I never thought I would see the day." Ian has to be careful as he remembers the first days. Even now, he can feel his heart race at the fun they expected to have.
But it was harder than you thought. You were misinformed.
"The movies made it seem easy. Much easier than this."

Mistakes I Made During the Zombie Apocalypse

Tell them the first mistake you made. The big one. The start of it all.
"I will in the morning. I'm tired."

• • •

In his dreams, Ian is in the closet examining old Polaroids from a shoe box when something large bumps against the closet door. He drops the photographs and listens to the soft sound of bare feet slowly shuffling on the wooden floor of the bedroom. The noise grows distant and then close until the thing slams into the closet door once more.

Is it alive or dead? Ian wonders.

In the door there is a keyhole, small in reality, but expansive in the dream world. When Ian looks through it he can see the entire bedroom and the thing pacing there. He pulls his eye away.

Ripley's corpse is walking back and forth from the edge of the bed and straight into the door. He forces himself to look through the keyhole again and when he does, the severed stumps of her fingers are all he can see. They no longer squirt blood; not even a drop falls from her dead body.

How did she get here?

As soon as Ian thinks it, Ripley's corpse changes course slightly, allowing Ian to see the middle of the four-poster bed. There on its bare mattress lies a familiar baby doll, a baby monitor still duct taped to its tiny plastic head. The bed catches fire, the baby doll melts and Ian can feel the heat build in the closet.

Keller.

• • •

The vivid dream, the heat of the fire still in his mind, Ian is nervous and covered in sweat when he wakes up in the closet. He checks for the shoe box, but it doesn't exist. He braves opening the door.

Sunlight fills the room and for the first time in months, apart from his fever and the passionate time he spent in bed with Ripley, warmth fills his body. She, of course still trapped in a shipping container, is not pacing the floor. The bed is empty. The mostly abandoned house smells worse than ever, but Ian is so relieved to be alone, it doesn't bother him.

I told you that talking about everything would make things better.
"This was my idea." Ian says. He walks to a window and lets the sunlight fall on his face.
Then you know you aren't done yet.
"Yeah," he says with a sigh. "None of this would have happened, except that…"

...I GLAMORIZED THE APOCALYPSE

Grant and Ian often talked about their plans for the zombie apocalypse. In a world where most every move of theirs was dictated or determined by an adult, it was fun to ponder survival and a life without rules. They read gun magazines, but never made it to the range. Ian's father was also scared of guns. Grant's dad couldn't be trusted with a weapon, even if he had been around. As a nurse, Ian's mother had seen firsthand what guns did to bodies; there was no way in hell that she'd allow them near one. Instead, they played first person shooting games to practice their aim.

They haunted the dehydrated food section of the sporting goods store, seeking new products to try. When his allowance allowed, Ian would buy a few of the plastic bags. Then he and Grant would spend a weekend taste testing as they dreamed about the abandoned houses they could inhabit when the world ended, larger and more lavish than their own.

• • •

Like this house.
"No, nothing like this shithole. All the good houses are ruined."
Even your own.
"It's good that it got burned down. It was about to be destroyed from the inside anyway."
The divorce.
"When Grant and I were gathering supplies, I found the paperwork on my mom's desk."
Irreconcilable differences.
"That's an understatement. The world ended and they went to their jobs across the infected city from one another. And they never once tried to make it back. Not even to me."

• • •

139

Before the zombies actually existed, Ian and Grant sat at the mall, watching people, pretending they were mindless and dead.

"That man, over by the piercing kiosk," Grant would start.

Ian would find the appointed victim and describe the ghastly wound he had suffered that brought about his demise. "His left arm is torn off at the elbow. The infection started there. He died of blood loss and came back."

"We could use the janitor's mop," Grant would continue. "Maybe sneak by the zombie and head into the knife shop to sharpen the handle into a spear."

"Why not just use something from the knife shop itself as the weapon?" Ian might ask.

"That's obvious. We need to challenge ourselves. There won't be weapons lying around in the event of a real zombie apocalypse."

"Right," Ian would agree. "Even the security guard's gun would be empty by the time we could take it."

"Most mall guards don't have guns," Grant would point out.

"Only stupid batons and handcuffs," Ian would realize.

• • •

You used to be so good at finding weapons.

"Kind of. Grant was always more creative."

Now that we've gone over the story, he was better at most things.

"Why the fuck are you saying things like that? I brought you here to help me!"

It's called tough love.

"And now that I'm listening, you won't shut up. I can't hide from you."

You can't hide from anything.

• • •

"Behind the Starbucks counter," Grant had once suggested. They would pick places to hide until it was safe to come out and explore.

"Under a pile of clothes from the racks at JC Penney," Ian said.

But none of it felt real. The games weren't desperate enough.

It was all talk, just talk.

They wished for it to happen as they watched one Romero flick after another. They played video games where they could build any weapon they wanted and where ammo and first aid kits littered the city.

A plague so great it would destroy nations; *that* was the plague of their dreams. And it was a plague that they were going to survive together. They wished for it.

• • •

Boy, did you ever get what you wished for!
"Part of it anyway."
You were fooled like the rest of the world when it started, though.

• • •

When it started, Ian thought it was bird flu; or swine flu, or mad cow disease, or anything other than the zombie apocalypse. The CDC reported it, but after their previous marketing campaign that featured zombies, few took them seriously. He laughed at the news anchors tossing the word 'zombie' around as though it was a possibility. The news anchors laughed too.

He wrote off the random attacks as drug fits and his mom and dad, who both saw a lot of folks on drugs, agreed. But as drugs tests came back negative, the medical world was running out of reasons.

And when they actually believed it was happening, their reaction was excitement. The boys wanted to get outside and play like children off of school due to snow, to get in the middle and prove themselves as fit to survive.

• • •

You prepared for a completely different end-of-days.
"A far more splendid one, ripe with ammo, food, and weapons."
A showdown in which Grant and you were bigger, stronger, more determined.
"And much less terrified."
Now that you see the mistakes you made, would you change them if you could?
"Hindsight is 20/20, but even though I see the mistakes I made,

I can't imagine that I would have the strength to do things differently if I had the chance. It would still be me. At some point I was bound to screw up. Grant, too cool to live, was doomed to die. And I, I would end up alone in the zombie apocalypse. 'You can't do anything right.' Grant said this to me once after I broke his skateboard while attempting a trick I knew I couldn't pull off. It hurt to hear him say that because it was an accurate observation, a definite fact. And Grant *still* chose to come to my house on the first day of infection. That was perhaps his one mistake in life, keeping a screw-up for a best friend. I won't find an uninfected girl or a gun (with any ammo), I won't go out in a blaze of glory (I'm too chickenshit to attempt it). I'm not even sure I can go downstairs again. Grant and Lena's bodies are still there. I may have to jump out of the window and attempt a safe landing like Ms. Kitty. It would be best if that didn't end as well."

What are your options?

"Stay here in this closet and say farewell to my respiratory and general health; inhaling particles from disintegrating clothing and watching the fleas get fatter on my blood under the dimming beam of my flashlight?"

The batteries won't last forever.

"Wait for Keller to decide to burn down the house with me in it?"

Death by fire is not advisable, but Lena's razor blade is still downstairs.

"Is suicide by rusted blade more advisable?"

Just one little cut is all you'd need. Otherwise you'll starve.

"And wait until the bodies and the world below me rot away?"

There is not one shred of glamour in that. But your story doesn't end here, in this house.

"No, not inside of it. Not on the front lawn. Maybe at the sidewalk, I can't be sure because the end of my story hasn't happened yet."

Still plenty of time to make more mistakes.

"At least one more. I'm sitting here wondering…"

...DID I WAIT TOO LONG TO MOVE ON?

Ian hears voices. More voices than his own. There are people outside. Real, living people, not the dead ones. He wants nothing more than to talk to them, to see faces that respond. He wants to be alive with them.

He has tried many times before to find the courage to stand up and make that next, most difficult decision, the decision to leave. But things have become comfortable to him in his uncomfortable closet in his mostly abandoned house.

"My legs are too weak," Ian whines to himself.
They can still carry you.
"The voices have faded. I'll never catch up," he cries.
You have to try! his mind screams.
"Move! Move!" Ian yells aloud. "Get the fuck out of this place!"
I think you're ready to tell this story as your own now...

• • •

My knees and back ache from the wood floor of the closet and I can barely pull myself to my feet. I feel as though I might have petrified if I'd stayed there an hour or two longer. Even though I've lost so much weight that my pants are threatening to leave my hips with every step, the floorboards still creak under my feet as I hobble to my backpack. I stare at Grant's bag; still in the center of the monument I built, though slightly askew from digging for the beans. I leave it there. It feels right, like a tombstone atop a grave, a testament to his existence and his death below.

My belongings packed, the few items I have left to my name, I head to the top of the stairs. Here, the bile rises in my throat for the smell of decay is too strong. I hold it down as I descend into the deepest pit of my own personal hell. Grant's body blocks my path. It is a writhing puddle of goo, flies and maggots. There are so many of the wriggling things that I can hear them devouring him. Smudges of blood shaped like the long back legs of a rabbit lead the way into the kitchen, but I don't have time to seek him.

I have to cross this rushing river of red and rot.

"Come on, it's just a bit of goo." Grant would say that to me. He was never squeamish.

I raise my left leg and the foot finds a bare spot of wood floor. The other leg follows, but the foot on its end slips on the rot. I fall down and end up lying face to face with the mess that is Grant. The vomit I suppressed on the stairs, which is mostly stomach acid seeing as how my belly is empty, comes rushing up my esophagus and onto him. It hardly makes a difference.

"If I leave the house, I won't be able to take you with me, Grant." I don't know why I'm telling him this, especially since I'm sobbing so hard my words can't be deciphered. Especially since he is dead.

"I'm sorry, Grant. You have to stay here," I say as I wipe the mess from my chin. "This is goodbye, again. Forever." I pull myself off of the slippery floor and walk the remainder of the hall. I pay no mind and bid no farewell to Lena's body as I pass the living room. I hope she is rotting in hell as much as she is rotting here.

I open the front door without first looking outside. Nothing is going to stop me from getting to these people. Whoever they are. Wherever they are going. Whatever I have to do.

This could be a trick. I have a brief moment of doubt as my feet leave the deck and tromp through the grass. It could be Keller. He carefully constructed attacks before. Hell, I hope it's him. One of us needs to die. We can't exist in this new world together.

Beyond the shade of the big tree in the yard, the sunlight is so bright that I have to hold an arm to my eyes to protect them. My closet was cavelike and my body was already starting to adapt to the deprivation of that place. After they adjust I can make out the group of survivors walking down the street. There is a little boy who holds the hand of a man, perhaps a father and son. Next to them another man, bearded and carrying a gun. Behind him, two women, one of which is armed as well. A Golden Retriever runs circles around the group until it sees me. Then it stops and wags its tail as it stares in my direction. The people stop too and look where the dog is looking, right at me. I can tell, by their hardened expressions and cautious steps, that the dog's enthusiasm does not extend to the humans that accompany it. The bearded man is most skeptical, as evidenced by his now raised gun, pointed at my head. I must look like death. I know that I feel like it.

I stumble toward them, hoping this isn't another mistake I'm making in the zombie apocalypse.

ABOUT THE AUTHOR

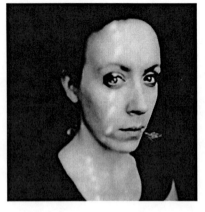

Michelle Kilmer is a horror enthusiast from Seattle, WA. When she is not writing, she enjoys hiking and camping, playing guitar, lifting weights, dressing up in "full gore" to attend zombie-related events, web design and gaming. Her writing portfolio also includes the novel When the Dead, the novel The Spread: A Zombie Short Story Collection, and a writing collection entitled Last Night While You Were Sleeping. Several of her short stories can be found in other books including Roms, Bombs, and Zoms from Evil Girlfriend Media, GIVE: An Anthology of Anatomical Entries from WtD Books, and A Very Zombie Christmas from ATZ Publications.

After many adventures and mistakes, she currently lives in Mill Creek, WA with her twin sister, two attack cats, and a broken heart.

ABOUT WHEN THE DEAD BOOKS

When the Dead Books is a small book company run by owner and author Michelle Kilmer. We bring horror, sci-fi, and fantasy fiction from indie writers to you. Check out our complete catalog at whenthedead.com.

MORE FROM WHEN THE DEAD BOOKS

WHEN THE DEAD

There is no way out for the residents of Willow Brook Apartments. Outside a plague is spreading while behind the walls, neighbors are forced to become friends…or enemies.

When the Dead…will introduce you to a doomed family, a dying child, an egomaniac, a murderer, and many other undesirables (including the undead!!) in three floors of secured-access chaos.

THE SPREAD

You don't know when it will change your life, or how, but the zombie plague is spreading quickly and in ways that no one could have imagined.

Featuring short stories that showcase the many ways in which a disease can overwhelm a city, The Spread will get you thinking of how mundane acts can become deadly.

GIVE: AN ANTHOLOGY OF ANATOMICAL ENTRIES

Have you ever loved someone so much, you'd give your left eye for them? Does two of a kind mean one to spare? Are *you* an organ donor?

GIVE: An Anthology of Anatomical Entries explores, from head to toe, the varying reasons why and how someone might donate an organ. Horror, Science Fiction, and dark humor blend in this collection.

LAST NIGHT WHILE YOU WERE SLEEPING

Displacement, replacement, injection, rejection, the best and the worst birthdays ever, vengeful spirits, disgruntled bridge trolls, a semi-sappy Satan, Bloody Mary as you've never seen her, Bigfoot, a suburban brush with the undead, rainbows you don't want to find the end of, and more. This collection includes mostly dark and sometimes humorous poetry, flash fiction, and short stories from Michelle Kilmer.

whenthedead.com   facebook.com/whenthedead   @whenthedead